It was only a matter of time

The general's troops were combing the jungle, moving through the scrub in tight formation to flush them out. Barrabas and O'Toole were back to back, shrouded by foliage not much greener than the camouflage paint on their faces.

O'Toole sighted thoughtfully along his gun before speaking. "Colonel," he intoned in a flat voice.

"What is it?" Barrabas snap-aimed his Beretta, then lowered it. He knew what was coming.

"I think we might be about to buy it." The words had barely left O'Toole's mouth before the steady *switch switch* noise intensified in the distance. It sounded like the rhythmic flicking of a fan—a fan whose blades were getting closer and closer.

SOLDIERS OF BARRABAS

SOLDIERS OF BARRABAS

THE BARRABAS FIRE

JACK HILD

A GOLD EAGLE BOOK FROM
WORLDWIDE.

TORONTO • NEW YORK • LONDON • PARIS
AMSTERDAM • STOCKHOLM • HAMBURG
ATHENS • MILAN • TOKYO • SYDNEY

First edition September 1989

ISBN 0-373-61632-5

Special thanks and acknowledgment to
Rich Rainey for his contribution to this work.

1

Drunken voices infiltrated the dreams of the sleeping villagers.

The Indian Ocean surf hissed soothingly at it rolled against the white sandy beach that had known no violence for more than fifty years. It was a dreamy sound, but it was a sound slowly being eaten away by the walking nightmares in khaki.

They spoke Swahili and they spoke loudly.

Their foreign voices were fueled by alcohol and smoke, and they made no attempt to hide their presence on the smallest of the populated islands in the Kormorelles chain.

Here, miles away from the endless light of the resort hotels on the main island, there was darkness. And in darkness there was comfort.

The men who approached over the sand had spent much of their careers in darkness, whether it was the actual cover of night or the official blanket of darkness their powerful paymasters could cast over their activities long after the damage was done.

The Tanzanian troops had been hiring out their talents for years now, occasionally picking up some military skills, but relying overall on their instincts.

They were a free-lance terror outfit whose main talent lay in the fact that there were no limits to what they would do. They were capable of anything, and they enjoyed their work.

Because of that, they were one of several mercenary groups imported to the islands to work for General Zahim, the new ruler of the Kormorelles, whose first act after leading a successful coup against his half brother had been to promote himself from lieutenant to general.

The Tanzanians had worked for a dozen generals like him before. They didn't care about his self-promotions or even his "liberation" policies, and some of them didn't really care about his money.

Besides, they weren't directly working for the general. They'd been recruited by the general's military adviser, a Frenchman who formerly served as a captain with 2e REP, the Second Foreign Legion Parachute Regiment.

A cool breeze fluttered around the huts, stirring up the ashes from the dead fire in the center of the village. It was ringed by a circle of smooth stones.

The leader of the Tanzanians, who signed his contracts with Europeans as Jean Blanc, staggered around the stones. A head taller than the others, he set the example for the troops in everything—drinking, fighting, rape and plunder.

He looked at the huts that were spread in a half circle facing the sea, then he smiled like a man who had just set foot into paradise.

The momentary quiet that had fallen over Blanc's troops ended when he pointed toward the target hut that housed tonight's entertainment.

The thatched dwelling housed a man and woman who had scoffed at General Zahim's team of negotiators who visited them two days earlier to discuss a tariff of fish and fruit, as well as the number of villagers that would be conscripted into the NKA, the New Kormorelles Army.

The villagers had chased them away, and the negotiators had withdrawn without incident. But tonight the negotiations would continue.

The first talks were one-sided, as the voices of the Tanzanians grew urgent. Most of the troops spoke a Swahili dialect, but some of them were native island enforcers who spoke the mixture of French and English left behind by their colonizers over the past few centuries.

Befitting a versatile leader, Blanc spoke French, English and Swahili. He'd robbed and murdered in several tongues.

Blanc led his men in a drunken march around the seaside hut, slowly tightening the circle like a noose. They kicked up sprays of sand against the thin walls of the hut, and it sounded like the breath of a hissing dragon.

From the outside the hut looked just like its neighbors, but the inhabitants were different from the rest.

The woman was a prized beauty of the village, and along with her husband, she was outspoken and blunt. Besides scoffing at the general's negotiators, she had mocked Zahim, saying that she was more of a general than he was.

Now the soldiers of the night had come to say their piece.

Along with their ubiquitous machetes, they carried AK-47s, M-16s, handguns, whatever they had been able to take from the well-stocked armory on the main island of the Kormorelles.

A sudden scuffling sound came from the hut to their left. It was the soft footpads of bare feet. Then came a pair of eyes peering briefly through the window before dropping out of sight.

Jean Blanc nodded at a burly soldier behind him. The man stepped out of sight, then crouched and sidled up to the hut and waited.

The face peered again.

THOCK!

The rifle butt smashed through the window and crashed into flesh and bone, shattering cartilage.

There was a scream of pain. After the sound of a falling body came the muffled sound of someone trying to quiet the person who'd been hurt.

A muted chorus of surprised voices and the sudden gasps of a defenseless people woken from sleep by armed prowlers issued from within the other huts.

There was movement inside the target hut, too, and panicked whispering.

It was time. Jean Blanc ducked and pushed through the doorway. He carried an AK-47 that looked almost like a toy in his huge hands.

Several other troops crashed in behind him, but they immediately fell silent, savoring the terror of the man and woman who were sitting up in bed.

Just into her twenties, a gorgeous full-breasted islander, the naked woman was clutching a sheet to herself in an attempt to cover her nudity.

The bed was on wooden stilts a foot off the ground. And below the bed was a long curved knife.

The man was trying to edge forward so he could grasp the knife, but he stopped halfway. There was precious little willingness or sense in fighting several automatic rifles with a steel blade.

"What do you want?" he finally asked. He helped cover his wife with a brightly colored blanket. Trying to size up the situation, he looked first into Blanc's eyes, then into the eyes of the rest of the intruders.

Although some of the soldiers were obviously islanders, there was no quarter in their eyes. The rogue islanders had found their calling with the terror squad.

Outside was the murmuring and pounding of the sea, the soothing sound they had grown so used to. Inside, the blood roared, pounding like jackhammers to head and heart.

Blanc pointed at the man with the barrel of his AK-47. "You," he said. "Out." He spoke English in a guttural manner that was accented by the rifle that swung crazily in a wide arc. He was drunk but acted drunker. "Now!" he slurred. "Out of here."

"No," the man said. "You can't touch her..." He reached for his blade and then hurtled forward, curling his right arm in front of him ready to make a killing slash.

A burst of 7.62 mm slugs met him halfway, chopping him to pieces from breastbone to head. Jean Blanc blew off the entire 30-round clip, making the dead man dance backward, his facial features splattered into an unrecognizable mass of bullet-torn flesh.

He landed in a heap, a wet, ruined mass of blood.

"Looks like we can touch her after all," Blanc said. He handed his AK-47 to one of his soldiers and took an AK-47 with a full clip in exchange.

The woman shrank from him. She was in shock from the destruction of the man who used to be her husband, a man who literally went to pieces in front of her.

"Please," she said, still clutching the blanket and sheet.

Blanc shook his head.

"We're all out of *please*," he said. He pressed the barrel of the AK-47 against her neck, tilting her backward and imprinting a mark from the barrel on her light skin.

The pressure forced her back onto the bed.

"We got no choice in the matter," Blanc continued. "No one does."

He drew the barrel down her breastbone, slowly pulling the sheet along with it.

"You know," he said, almost conversationally, "we didn't come for your body, not exactly. But we'll take it of course. See, what we really came here for was your mind. You and everyone else in the village.''

Blanc nosed the barrel of the AK under the blanket and sheet, then unhurriedly drew them down.

He made a game of it. The barrel of the AK-47 inched the sheet down, revealing her bare skin—and the sharp blade she held in her right hand.

It slashed upward, going straight for Jean Blanc's chest. But her hand ran into a steel wall as Blanc's large fingers coiled around her wrist. He twisted it sharply.

The knife dropped from her hands, she fell onto the bed, and he threw himself on top of her.

Jean Blanc took her body and soul. Then he stepped outside, making way for the rest of his troops.

Weeks ago they'd been marauding through Tanzanian slums, taking down whoever and whatever came their way, while they waited for some work to come along. Today they were in uniform. Today they were soldiers in the New Kormorelles Army, whisked away from East Africa and flown into the islands as a cargo of licensed killers.

Standing in the moonlight, Jean Blanc conducted the exercise in terror by dispatching several of his soldiers to prowl noisily around some of the other huts.

By then, many of the villagers were pouring out of their huts, realizing that the midnight invaders weren't going to leave *them* alone.

They were met by AK-47s.

The soldiers opened up on them indiscriminately, the lightning bursts of their automatic rifles searing through the darkness.

Two women and a teenage boy ran down toward the beach, the sand spraying behind them as their heels dug in for dear life. The women's braided hair bounced like horse tails as they raced for freedom.

Four khaki-clad men chased after them, unable to suppress their excitement at the new challenge. Firing from the hip, they poured full-auto bursts into the fleeing villagers.

Their prey tumbled forward awkwardly, lifted off their feet in a grotesque dance that shredded their flesh and tossed them onto the sand.

The scene was repeated all across the village, as the fleeing natives fell to the ground, their legs shot out from under them.

The soldiers finished some of them off and let others roll around on the ground in agony. A number of villagers stayed put, crouched in terror as lead fusillades ripped through their huts. Screams and tears and blood colored the night.

The terror lasted for two hours. The NKA troops had nothing to fear. The island police force had been given strict orders to stay on the main island for the night.

When the slaughter was finally finished and the troops were sated, Jean Blanc himself torched the hut where the first man and woman they had visited lay together, now wedded in death.

With the hut burning like a beacon behind them, the troops jogged for the jeeps they'd left a mile away.

Behind them the groans and half-mad cries of the survivors gave tortured witness that the night's mission was a total success.

2

Nile Barrabas opened the door to nowhere at 1600 hours.

It was the jump door of an experimental airplane, a tilt-rotor V-22 Osprey that hovered above the middle of the Indian Ocean thousands of miles away from any of the world's major powers.

But it was only a hundred miles away from the paranoia-racked paradise of the Kormorelles island chain.

Blood drenched the white sand beaches, courtesy of the coup that ousted the islanders' playboy king. The Emperor of Ecstasy, as Jamal Daoud had been mockingly referred to, had been toppled by his half brother, a so-called military man named General Zahim.

Shock waves of slaughter spread from island to island as the beardless general solidified his hold.

But he didn't know that time had run out. New players, the Soldiers of Barrabas had come on to the scene.

Once they'd arrived at the drop zone, the Osprey hovered above the water high enough so the down wash from the prop rotors wouldn't create a hazard for the disembarking team.

Designed for special operations and search-and-rescue missions, the Osprey had enough fuel to travel a thousand nautical miles away from its warship and still carry teams and equipment.

Officially conducting a test run, the aircraft's true mission was to drop off the team of mercenaries led by ex-Special Forces colonel Nile Barrabas.

The man with the distinctive shock of nearly white hair—scorched white by the fires he'd traveled through these past two decades—was known by sight to only a relative few, inside or outside the covert chain of command.

The same held true for the men and one woman who made up the small contingent known as the Soldiers of Barrabas, or as they preferred to think of themselves, the SOBs.

Though they were a ghost army, the mercenaries cast a long shadow wherever they went into action. Right now that shadow was part of the Osprey, whose rippling silhouette masked the bright diamond-capped waves of the Indian Ocean cresting below them.

Barrabas scanned the horizon. There was nothing in sight. No sign of any other human.

"Welcome to your new home," Barrabas said to the stick of five mercenaries lined up behind him.

Each mercenary wore a black wet suit and life jacket, and a web belt containing survival gear.

Barrabas tapped the first merc, a tough Greek seaman named Alex Nanos.

"Go," Barrabas said.

Nanos went.

With the straps of his fins and face mask looped around his right arm, the Greek mercenary gripped the metal bar that extended a few feet out from the Osprey. Like a kid on a trapeze bar, he swung out over the water. Angling his feet forward, Nanos let go of the bar. Once he was airborne, he clutched fins and face mask to his chest and splashed down.

When he surfaced, he put on his fins and waited for the rest of the troops. One by one the others followed suit.

With the SOBs in position, the loading ramp of the Osprey dropped down and two IBS (Inflatable Boat Small) crafts were lowered on winch lines. The inflatable boats were loaded with sophisticated equipment and weaponry they were bringing with them on their sojourn into paradise.

Each IBS could carry seven men and one thousand pounds of cargo. Splitting up with three members to each inflatable, the SOBs managed to bring in a few extra items that might mean the difference between life and death.

Strapped in beneath the tarps was as much equipment and supplies the SOBs could bring in with them from the outside world. Any resupply mission was far off in the future and in fact was highly questionable. When the fireworks went off, the powers that be intended to be as far removed from the SOBs as possible.

Floating alongside the inflatables, the SOBs removed the winch lines, unwrapped the tarps, and then climbed aboard. Each inflatable had a silent-running outboard motor, although out there in the middle of nowhere, silence wasn't a key issue.

Survival was, however, a key issue, especially since the royal yacht that was supposed to meet them was nowhere in sight.

"Where the hell is King Tut and company?" Nanos asked, holding on to the steering bracket of the 7.5 HP engine. The weathered Greek raised his hand to shadow his eyes, looking as if he were saluting the endless horizon as he scanned it for the yacht's silhouette.

"King Daoud," Barrabas said. "And obviously something's detained them." He thought of the oceangoing yacht that carried the island's last hope for freedom. "Maybe the weather," he said. "Or maybe a bad case of lead poisoning."

There was a strong chance of the latter, Barrabas thought. Deposed rulers were positively magnetic when it came to attracting gunfire.

ONE MAN HAD STAYED behind in the Osprey, looking down at the SOBs, who were already piloting their inflatables in the direction of the Kormorelles, drifting up and down in the swells of the waves.

Despite his considerable bulk, the man who observed the start of the mission from his high vantage point was Walker Jessup, one of the world's foremost shadowy operators.

Widely known as The Fixer, he had a talent for obscuring the real backers of SOB missions.

Walker Jessup had brokered the deal between the cashiered king and his crackerjack commando squad. They were not really his, though. He could count on them only when the mission was "clean."

And though the real backer of the mission was the United States, Jessup had engineered matters so the king thought it was *his* idea to employ the SOBs. And since Daoud was credited with the idea, it was only natural that he pay the considerable fees of the SOBs—an amount large enough to pay a small army, which was exactly what they were.

The king could afford it, however. Like many a fallen ruler, Daoud had managed to hold on to the purse strings of power. He had huge reserves stashed away in overseas banks for those inevitable rainy days of revolution.

All told, the king would be shelling out in excess of three million for importing the SOBs and their warmaking machinery. But they were worth every last bloodred cent.

Jessup had worked with Nile and his crew for years now. The former CIA operator had first hooked up with Barrabas in Nam where they were both plying their trade. Jessup as spymaster, Colonel Barrabas as master soldier.

They'd worked well together, and as they prospered, their reputation grew.

Barrabas had assembled a first-class crew, each individual capable of running a mercenary outfit themselves. Working together under Barrabas, it was like having an all-star team.

But it wasn't sport they excelled at—it was war.

And the goal was freedom.

Jessup closed the door on the SOBs, then sat down in his seat and fastened his safety belt.

A year or two ago the belt might not have encompassed his mass so easily, but lately he'd been waging a guerrilla war against his former size.

Sometimes he won the skirmishes of the weight wars, other times he went on a binge and ballooned up to his former scale-shattering weight.

That weight had been steadily, pound by pound, removing him from the active mercenary world over the years. And that bulk almost guaranteed that he would never go back into the field.

It was also a pretty good guarantee that sooner or later he would be removed from any kind of work unless he shaped up. Or down. Whatever it took to get back into the swing of things.

He'd seen it happen to other old soldiers in Washington. Men whom once he'd considered invulnerable, suddenly went to pot, pills, booze or the wrong kind of women, and then they were gone.

Out of control.

Out of power.

Many of his contacts in the Washington power parade were getting too old for the job or were being pushed out of office by eager, younger aspirants.

There was a lot to be said for that, because so many of those contacts had sold out Jessup and the SOBs time after time. It was usually a matter of politics or economics, which when you came down right to it were pretty much the same thing in Washington.

In recent years, however, Jessup had cultivated solid relations with a covert controller in the NSA, Theodore Nicholas, known as Tsar Nicholas because of his inexhaustible knowledge of his Russian opponents. And though he had the mannerisms and intellect of a cultured professor, Tsar Nicholas had the instincts of a soldier. Instincts that had been molded by a career in the Navy.

Second in command to DIRNSA, the Director of the NSA, Tsar Nicholas controlled his empire from his office on Mahagony Row, in the upper reaches of the Puzzle Palace at Fort Meade, Maryland.

In a way it was Tsar Nicholas who was responsible for the SOBs being out there in the middle of nowhere. The NSA had just about cemented a deal with King Daoud to establish an NSA monitoring station on one of the Kormorelles. Then the revolution happened.

The general, who had quietly built up his own fortune over the years, suddenly put that fortune to use, purchasing the throne with an army of soldiers of fortune. Overall they were nothing like Barrabas and his SOBs. The general's soldiers of fortune were the animal kind. The kind who were soldiers in name only.

They were the type who could conduct a genocidal war against the king's supporters—and be surprised that they were getting paid for having so much fun.

The rampage they went on turned into an ongoing bloodbath that showed no sign of stopping.

Until now.

The Soldiers of Barrabas would soon be on the scene in the Kormorelles, and Walker Jessup would be working behind the scenes in Pine Gap, Australia, where the NSA ran one of its largest and most well-known top-secret bases in the world.

A crewman came back to see if The Fixer, the man who officially wasn't there, was ready to go.

Jessup nodded his head.

The Osprey rose, the tilt-rotors angled into horizontal mode, and headed for the U.S. Navy cruiser that would take Walker Jessup to the land down under.

LIGHTS GLIMMERED on the horizon, gradually coming closer as the royal yacht cut through the darkness and headed for the two inflatable boats riding the waves.

The green flashing light from one of the boats sometimes disappeared in the deep troughs between the waves, but the yacht easily zeroed in on it.

It was a hundred and forty-three footer, more a ship than a yacht. In King Daoud's glory days, the yacht had been the unofficial cruise liner for the Hollywood celebrities who descended upon the islands. The floating palace had been graced by all of the glorious names around. King Daoud himself personally entertained the actresses, taking them into his fold, then into his bed.

It had been a yacht fit for a king.

But for this cruise it was somewhat stripped down. Instead of gala party lights, it was rigged with spotlights. And now it was stocked with as many guns as it had fishing gear.

Unquestionably the pursuit of pleasure was giving way to the pursuit of power.

The yacht anchored and waited for the approach of the inflatables. A three-man team under the supervision of a former SAS officer named Douglas Mann worked the large spotlights that tracked the approaching boats.

The inflatables came in slowly, making their way carefully through the waves which had gone from moderate to rough.

At one point the occupants of the boats began shouting with the wild enthusiasm of people who were overjoyed at being rescued from the sea. Their voices carried well, but sounded a bit muffled.

Then, just as suddenly as it began, the shouting stopped.

When the lead inflatable was thirty yards away, the spotlight revealed that there was only one man piloting it. The other shapes were piles of canvas and packs.

A second spotlight speared through the darkness, revealing that there was only one person manning the second boat also.

"Hold it right there!" Douglas Mann shouted through a megaphone. His British accent marked him as King Daoud's bodyguard, and his tone of voice also marked him as a man who was used to command.

When there was no response from the inflatables, Mann raised the megaphone again. "There were supposed to be six of you!" he shouted. "Where are the others?"

The Briton was about to grab his side arm when a calm voice answered behind him.

"Right here."

Mann turned around slowly and looked into the face of Barrabas.

He also looked at the US Navy Model 22 silenced 9 mm pistol the leader of the SOBs held in his hand.

The water still dripping down him, wearing a slick black wet suit, the mercenary held the stainless steel pistol casually in his hand, not in a threatening manner as if the other man's death was imminent. But even so, it was clear to Douglas Mann that if necessary he could be taken out in a split second.

Four times over.

Three other men in similar garb emerged from the shadows. One of them carried a rubber-sheathed grappling hook they'd used to board the yacht, the others carried the shallow-depth closed circuit scuba gear the team had used to swim over. Each man also carried a weapon like their leader.

Douglas Mann scanned the tableau before him, then said, "You fellows always drop in this way?"

"We come in whatever way we have to," Barrabas said. "We assumed your mission was compromised when you didn't show up on time."

"A breach of etiquette punishable by death," Mann said.

Barrabas shrugged. "No one here felt like getting shot up by a boatload of the general's yacht-jackers," he said, stepping closer to the Briton.

"And how do I know you're Barrabas?" Mann said. His hand still hovered near his side holster.

"If you know anyone else crazy enough to paddle around the middle of the ocean in a rubber tube, I'd like to meet him."

Mann's hand moved away from the holster.

He explained they were late because of the need to evade a small group of crafts that could have been the general's search party.

Mann was about Barrabas's height and maybe the same age. A lock of his brown hair coiled down his forehead. His hands, which he raised cautiously, were solid and weathered. He didn't lift them in abject surrender, but far enough away so they didn't present any immediate danger.

Barrabas stepped forward, disarmed him and handed the Browning to the black mercenary who had come up beside him.

The other mercenaries searched Mann's small welcoming committee and removed any weapons.

"We'd like to take a look around," Barrabas said.

"Perhaps you'd like to take a look at the king," Mann suggested.

The man was cool under fire and, under different circumstances, would have made more trouble for the SOBs. But concentrating on the two boats approaching from the front of the yacht, he hadn't expected a team to hit him from the side.

They'd obviously accomplished that feat while the two men in the inflatables were shouting out, covering any sound of their lethally silent approach.

"Okay," Barrabas said. "Let's take a look."

Mann glanced at *his* men who were standing idly by the spotlights, signaling that everything was okay and not to make any moves. They were more used to luxurious island hopping than a combat cruise.

Then he glanced meaningfully at the automatic in Barrabas's hand. "Do we get any last requests?"

"If the king is alive," Barrabas said, "then there's nothing to worry about. If this is some kind of trap..."

Mann stared back at him defiantly. "Yes?"

"Then your worries are over," Barrabas concluded.

The Briton nodded. He wasn't mad at the precautions Barrabas was taking. Rather he was annoyed with himself for letting down his guard. He'd expected someone good. Someone hard. And the man standing in front of him was evidence that they'd got what they were looking for.

"Let's get this out of the way now," Mann said, "so we can become friends before we kill each other."

Barrabas signaled to the SOBs in the inflatables. The mercs on board helped them tie up to the yacht and then lowered the access ladder, so they could come aboard in a more conventional manner.

Barrabas holstered the silenced automatic and defused the tensions of the yacht crew.

His instincts told him everything was safe. But there was always a chance that the Briton had thrown his lot in with the backers of the coup.

Bodyguards and security advisers were always targeted for payoffs. No matter how many times they saved their employer's life, there could always be a next time when they gave it away.

So it wasn't impossible that the king was now under guard or perhaps even dead, that a hit squad was just waiting to finish off the mercs.

It was a slim possibility, but Barrabas and the SOBs had stayed alive this long by reducing the odds against them every chance they got.

Douglas Mann led the way belowdecks to the king's stateroom and knocked on the door.

"Yes?" a relaxed voice cried out from inside.

"It's Douglas," Mann said.

"Are they here?"

Mann looked at the mercenaries who surrounded him.

"Very much so," he said.

Douglas opened the door, then started to escort the SOBs inside. But before Mann could enter, the black merc slipped in front of him and entered first. He quickly scanned the room before nodding back at Barrabas. The other SOBs entered with Douglas Mann, leaving damp footprints on the carpet as they flanked him on both sides.

Barrabas recognized the king. He looked a bit tougher than he'd been led to expect by his photographs. The society photos that were in the dossier all portrayed an easygoing man, someone who had gone out to pasture.

But King Daoud looked exceptionally fit. His hair was cut short, coming to a sharp peak above his forehead and giving him a predatory look. His light copper skin was unblemished, and his jaw was strong and clean shaven.

Barrabas assumed the playboy image was just that. An image, one of many the king could conjure up for the occasion. After all, the negotiations he conducted with the NSA had revealed a shrewd man who wasn't overwhelmed by the agency's high-tech wizards and warlocks.

One look around and it was obvious the king liked to surround himself with luxury. The stateroom was outfitted in baronial splendor. But it was geared to a futuristic baron. A pair of matching Flemish tapestries was separated by a huge curved silver screen, giving it the look of a small-scale drive-in. A large round bed that could accommodate a miniharem, and priceless works of art, took up most of the room. Sculpted wooden statues and jewel-encrusted icons were displayed around the room on heavy metal pedestals, a silent audience for the king.

It looked like a floating imperial treasury.

There were signs that a woman or two had recently been here. Veils and wispy silk garments left a trail across the bed.

The king was sitting on the edge, propped up by a makeshift throne of huge silk pillows.

After taking in the king's surroundings in a few moments, Barrabas stepped forward.

"King Daoud?" he said. It wasn't really a question. The man before him matched the photos and the life-style he'd been prepared for.

The king nodded.

"I'm Nile Barrabas."

"You are most welcome, Colonel Barrabas," he said. "And is this your army?" The king cast a skeptical eye on the six mercenaries who'd entered the room. "The fabled Soldiers of Barrabas."

"Fabled, maybe," Barrabas said. "I don't give a damn about that. But they sure as hell are extraordinary soldiers."

"I see," Daoud said. "Even so, you are but six…I don't see how you can do everything that this man Jessup claimed you can."

Mann cut in. "I think they will," he said.

The king nodded. Obviously he respected Mann's opinion. As the one who had kept him alive so far, it was definitely worth something.

But he'd apparently been spending a lot of time second-guessing the decisions he'd made. Still, there was no other recourse.

"About the claims Jessup made," Barrabas said. "If he told you we'd waltz right in and plunk you down on the throne, that's wrong. If he told you we'd set the stage and spearhead a countercoup—with your help—then he was right on target."

"I am interested in restoring a presidency, rather than retaking the throne," Daoud replied.

Barrabas nodded. Just before the coup, when some Kormorellois factions were clamoring for democracy, Daoud had obliged them by declaring himself president and changing his royal advisers to cabinet members.

Now he had the honor of being both an ex-king and an ex-president. As one who had experienced power and its decline, the man knew that anything could happen. Still, he was skeptical seeing the reality of the small force before him.

"If it will help," Barrabas said, "let me introduce my people."

The king shrugged. "It doesn't matter," he said, looking around at the assembly of soldiers of fortune. "I'm sure they're good."

"Good is not the word," Barrabas said. "But there's another reason. I want you and all your people to know their faces so no one goes around shooting at the wrong side."

"An excellent idea," the king said.

Barrabas extended his arm, then introduced the other Soldiers of Barrabas.

The black mercenary was Claude Hayes, a onetime specialist with the Navy's Underwater Demolition Teams. Along with leading assaults on beach and harbor installations for the Navy, Hayes had soldiered on his own, up and down the African continent, before he was recruited by Barrabas. The UDT spoke French, Swahili, and several other African dialects.

Alex Nanos, a Greek brawler and weight lifter who had been careful not to let bulk overwhelm his speed, was something of a ladies' man. He spoke Greek, Russian and German well, and cursed fluently in several other languages.

After being introduced, Nanos said, "So, Your Highness, where are all the chicks I been hearing about?"

Daoud laughed. "Oh, they are here, my friend. But when they heard you were coming, they asked to be put under lock and key."

Barrabas smiled. It appeared that the king had been briefed on his crew as thoroughly as Barrabas had been briefed on the king and his court.

The next SOB was Leona Hatton. Although Lee's dark hair was cut short to a fighting length, her hourglass figure camouflaged her abilities as a fighter. Born into a U.S. military family, she was at home in the covert world of the mercs.

The king looked hard and long at Lee Hatton. Finally he said, "A woman."

"A soldier," Lee said.

"Ahh, yes, a medic, is it—"

"A doctor."

"And, of course, a noncombatant."

Barrabas cut in. "When *she's* through with people, they often need a doctor. Since she's already there for them, it's like...killing two terrorists with one stone."

Barrabas then introduced the red-haired Irishman, Liam O'Toole, a decorated army captain and an undiscovered poet, whose verse was appreciated only by a small circle. As Nanos was fond of saying, he was well loved by those who weren't familiar with his work.

Despite his few brushes with publishers of subterranean poetry, O'Toole was still soldiering on, in both his crafts of epic poet and soldier. Each of his callings fueled the other—as did his fondness for drink. Between his assignments with the SOBs, O'Toole often boarded the whiskey train, prowling bars across the world on an endless quest for a topless muse.

The last SOB was William Starfoot II, the Osage Indian known as Billy Two. Marine veteran and martial artist, he was a master of guerrilla warfare. With his black hair pulled taut in a tail draped over his neck, he looked impressive, given his massive size and brooding presence.

Barrabas waved the Osage forward and said, "And this is—"

"We have already met," the king said.

Barrabas cocked his head. He looked first at the king, then at Billy Two. "Is that right?" he asked.

The Osage nodded.

"Yes," Daoud replied. "In another lifetime."

Barrabas didn't look surprised. He had been exposed to Billy Two enough so that any otherworldly claims did not take him aback.

"Then, for the here and now—"

"You are right," Daoud said in agreement. "What matters now, Barrabas, is that you and I discuss matters. If we could talk in private."

Barrabas nodded. "We'll stow our gear, and while my team is getting settled, you and I can have our talk."

"I look forward to it," Daoud said. "As I'm sure you know, you are my last hope."

Me and any good psychiatrist, Barrabas thought. But instead he nodded, then led his men out of the room.

Once out in the hallway, heading for their quarters, Barrabas turned to the Osage.

"That bit about him knowing you before, meeting you in the past," Barrabas said. "Did you feel the same thing?"

"I wasn't about to call a king a crock," Billy Two said.

"But about what he said..."

"I did think he looked familiar," Billy Two said. "His aura, that is."

Barrabas shrugged, though he knew that Billy Two's statements weren't all that facetious. For some time now he'd been grappling with an entity called Hawk Spirit, which the various members of the SOBs interpreted as a guardian angel, a channel, a deranged ghost, a spirit warrior, or a figment of his imagination. Billy Two's own interpretation of the entity that occasionally possessed or inspired him was constantly changing.

It first came about when he'd been captured by the Soviets on an earlier SOB mission and they'd injected him with drugs that had driven his mind to the very

limits of sanity. His recovery was slow and painful—
and not altogether complete.

And though it was a horrible experience, in many
ways it had helped Billy Two. There were a number of
times when, relying on his Hawk Spirit instincts—
whatever the source—Billy Two had pulled the SOBs
out of the fire.

And though none of the SOBs was much devoted to
any cult or religious idea—be it spirits or sprites—they
weren't about to dismiss anything that helped Billy
Two.

Except for Nanos, that is, who made it an avoca-
tion to needle the Osage who often cruised around
with him in the Florida Keys between their SOB operations.

Lately Nanos had started to call Hawk Spirit "Billy
Three."

As they reached the end of the long corridor, Barrabas clapped his hand onto Billy's shoulder and said,
"What's your gut feeling about the king?"

The Osage regarded Barrabas with a somber
expression, and said, "He's led an interesting life." He
paused for a moment, then added, "Or lives."

THE SCENT OF SANDALWOOD filled the air when Barrabas and Mann returned to the king's stateroom.
Mingling with the incense was the suggestion of a lingering perfume, but there was no sign of any woman.

Perhaps she was ensconced in one of the suites that
were connected to the stateroom, Barrabas thought.
Or perhaps she didn't exist at all. He pictured a har-

emless king releasing push-button perfume into the room to maintain his fabled reputation.

That didn't seem likely. Besides, Barrabas was quite sure he had heard some girlish laughter from one of the rooms along the corridor.

It was just possible that the rumors of the king's notorious appetites were true. But it was hard to tell from Daoud's cool, collected appearance as he sat calmly on the middle of three modular couches that formed a horseshoe shape around a well-stocked table.

Barrabas and Mann dropped onto opposite sides of the couch.

Though there was a wide array of drink and food set out on the table before them, Barrabas settled for a tumbler of whiskey and a cigar. As he exhaled the smoke, he saw it drawn upward, dispersed by a fan in the ceiling.

Mann lit up a pipe, as did the king.

When kings gather, Barrabas thought, amused at the way the three of them were puffing away like some council of wise old men.

The king began the briefing, speaking rapidly, sometimes appearing to surprise himself as he recounted the events that led up to the coup and its aftermath.

He had a photographic memory, often reciting word for word what he and others had said in earlier conversations, sometimes speaking their parts with great emotion. He was like a tribal storyteller, talking of a great kingdom. But now and then his eyes clouded as he looked into the future and saw that his very own personal epic could very well become a tragedy.

Though the hour was late, Daoud showed no sign of tiring. Periodically he called upon Mann to fill in some of the details.

Mann lacked the storytelling ability, and he wasted no words. He spoke in a precise, military manner.

Although much of the material was familiar from his previous talks with Jessup, Barrabas wanted a firsthand account, something that he could judge for himself.

The king spoke with some sadness of the changes he'd introduced to the Kormorelles, perhaps in hindsight regretting the speed with which they had been thrown inexorably into the twentieth century.

He also spoke candidly, aware that the United States' interest in the Kormorelles didn't stem from a fondness for its white sandy beaches.

The same location that made the Kormorelles attractive to the European colonizers, now made it a gem for the intelligence gatherers.

A group of American engineers had already made a preliminary site survey on the remote island that was selected to hold the base. Things had been going along smoothly until the coup.

The planned NSA listening post on the Kormorelles could serve as an anchor for the geosynchronous satellite systems vacuuming up communications over the Indian Ocean. A monitoring station on the Kormorelles could target Africa to the west, then sweep around to Saudi Arabia, Iran,

India, China, Russia, Indonesia, down to Australia on the east.

To the NSA it was an electronic paradise, especially with the constant shifting of hesitant allies who were fond of closing U.S. bases or extorting outrageous advantages from the U.S. to keep them in operation.

Barrabas knew a considerable amount about the negotiations for the NSA post. Though Daoud was pressing for a king's ransom, it wasn't nearly as extortionate as a number of U.S. allies were demanding for similar leasing rights.

King Daoud had been carefully cultivated over the years, and though he had shortcomings, like his predilection for squiring starlets and maintaining an elegant but unwieldy harem, he had a most important quality: he was a man the U.S. could deal with. To boot, he'd proved that he was a man of his word.

Unfortunately the word of an ex-king meant little when his land was ruled over by a tyrant-in-training who saw himself as a world leader. For his word to ever mean anything again, Daoud had to recapture the Kormorelles.

Barrabas sensed that there was more to it than a lust for the power and prestige the king once possessed. After all, he could quite easily go to Europe and live in a comfortable exile. But Daoud believed that he'd let down the islanders, failing them in shaping their destiny.

Therefore he was prepared to fight, and had been shocked when he found that his potential benefactors in the U.S could do nothing for him. Openly, that is. Clandestinely was apparently another matter altogether.

Daoud described to Barrabas his meeting with Jessup.

His contacts in the NSA put him in touch with the man called The Fixer, who arrived on the yacht's helipad in an unmarked, untraceable chopper when the king had been cruising just off the northern coast of Australia.

The king soon found that Jessup was a man whose appetites were nearly as voracious as his own, although the massive power broker from Washington appeared to be more interested in gastronomical delights than he was in Daoud's floating harem.

After the intimacy of sharing a minor feast with the king, Jessup had offered his services. The Fixer claimed to be in contact with an unofficial army that had done a lot of work for the West in the past.

Mann knew the score, and understood what was being offered right from the beginning. Rather than try and recruit his own mercenary outfit, Mann advised the king to opt for the help that was being steered his way, however indirectly, by the U.S.

"What can you do for me that the United States of America can't?" the king had asked.

"Would you like a battalion of U.S. Marines to storm the beaches of the Kormorelles?" Jessup had responded.

"Of course," the king replied. "But I understood that it was out of the question."

"It is," Jessup said. "But I've got the next best thing."

It was a battalion of six. The Soldiers of Barrabas.

"You come to me promising help and you offer me a force that is only six strong."

"The operational word here," Jessup had said, "is strong."

While not quite supermen, the six mercs had done this kind of work before—accomplished significant objectives against extraordinary odds. The fact that they were still alive had to mean something.

King Daoud negotiated a fee with The Fixer, transferred some of his millions to numbered Swiss accounts, and then waited for the cavalry to arrive.

Now, looking at Barrabas, the king smiled and said, "And then the cavalry came. They came underwater and in the dead of night."

"Right," Barrabas said. "And now the cavalry is ready to ride into battle. But first I want to know what resources you still have on the islands."

"There are some assets we can call upon," Mann said. "We've established a number of safehouses. And there are caches of money and weapons."

That was welcome news to Barrabas. The king hadn't gone into too much detail with Jessup. It was a natural precaution. Why show your hand to someone who might or might not be playing against you? However, now that the Soldiers of Barrabas had arrived, there was a chance to play that hand.

Barrabas bit into his cigar, then exhaled a gust of smoke. He said, "It's nice having safehouses and weapons. But it's even nicer if you have people to use them. Do you have any we can count on?"

Daoud nodded. "There are some who will fight when we call upon them. There are others who are waiting to see which way the battle goes. Right now it appears to be totally one-sided on Zahim's part. But if *someone* shows them that Zahim can be beaten, they will follow."

Mann and the king then gave Barrabas a crash course in the history and politics of the islands.

In turn Barrabas presented them with a number of military scenarios—instinctively turning to Mann for input on how the population would react.

As they talked late into the night, Barrabas pressed King Daoud and Mann to pinpoint other potential sources of help.

"There is one more possible source," Mann said.

Daoud looked askance at him. It was the first time that Barrabas had seen the king show displeasure with the Briton.

"There is?" Barrabas prodded, looking directly at the king.

"In a way," Daoud said. "There is a society among the out islanders. A brotherhood." The king shook his head. "But we've traveled different roads for far too long. I don't think they will offer much help to our cause."

"What is this brotherhood?" Barrabas asked.

"It's a religious society of warriors and priest-esses," Mann answered. "In some ways it's a *secret* society, although not too secret. They trace their ancestry to the ancient sky gods of the islands. Unfortunately their leader was assassinated by one of Zahim's death squads. As were most of their other leaders. Until a new leadership emerges, the society is effectively crippled.''

"Maybe,'' Barrabas said. "But if there is someone they respect—some warrior they can follow—do you think they will rise against Zahim?''

Mann looked hard at Barrabas. "They might just as easily fight us. It depends on who they choose as their leader.''

"I've got just the man,'' Barrabas said.

"Oh, really?'' Mann said. "You travel with a warrior priest?''

"You could say that,'' Barrabas answered, thinking of the Osage. "If this is a warrior cult, they'll be birds of a feather.''

3

The Kormorelles were a few islands from Eden that had splashed down into the world.

On a map the Kormorelles looked like specks of dust surrounded by an ocean of blue. Smack in the middle of the Indian Ocean, dwarfed to near invisibility by the distant landmasses north and south, east and west, the islands could easily be considered to be mistakes overlooked by the printer, a few scratch marks in the blue universe.

Lying north of the Madagascar-Mauritius-Australia axis, the Kormorelles had been a paradise found and lost over the past few hundred years. At various times it had been a fierce tribal confederation of headhunters, a stronghold for pirates, and a way station for some of the ships plying the sea, a place where they could resupply their water and take on fruits to keep their crews free from scurvy. And now and then they sparked a few wars with the natives by taking some of the native women aboard.

The Kormorelles were on the Dutch route from the Cape of Good Hope to Java and the other Indonesian islands.

They were also on the routes used by African, English, French and Chinese traders.

Stops were made by the dhows of Arabic merchants who brought Chinese and Southeast Asian luxuries to East Africa, and sailed back with treasures of every kind, ranging from gold to ivory to human cargo.

As a result, the natives had assimilated the cultures of each, finally blending into a largely English- and French-speaking colonial outpost with an Arabic and African heritage.

Eventually the Kormorelles became a colony of the Europeans, traded, fought over, won and lost by the Dutch, English and French, changing hands a number of times before finally achieving independence in the nineteenth century.

Since then the islands had gone unheralded, governed by a succession of kings, until the late seventies when they began to attract the attention of a different kind of colonizers. Resort developers moved into the islands, making it a paradise for tourists—and for King Daoud, who luxuriated in the attention and the wealth lavished upon him.

There were still several factions of islanders who wanted to hold on to the kind of life their families had lived for hundreds of years. They wanted freedom to govern their own tribal affairs, freedom to continue the quiet pastoral life. Fishing, farming, and keeping alive the tradition surrounding the rich pantheon of island gods took up most of their time.

King Daoud wisely made several of the islands off-limits to the developers so the villages could continue as before.

He created several ministries to put the wealth that came into the islands to good use. But he didn't regulate them all that well. As long as he lived like a king, he assumed everyone else was doing just fine.

The ministries gradually came under the influence of his half brother, who had diverted to his use many of the funds earmarked for the islanders, creating a growing gulf between the poor and the wealthy.

The population had increased so that the Kormorellois could no longer support themselves solely from the local resources. There were locally grown foods—as well as the harvest from the sea—but more and more they relied on imported goods.

Imports that didn't quite get to all of them.

After creating the appearance of a class of wealthy overlords and starving villagers, Zahim led a revolution to crush the very conditions he'd started. To do that, he sent a large army—by Kormorellois standards—to take over the seats of power.

His band of thugs, the NKA, seized the airport, the radio station, the hydropower installation and the official buildings housing the king's ministers.

The army was composed of foreign mercenaries and turncoat islanders who overwhelmed the island militia with only a few casualties, then incorporated them into units commanded by ruthless mercenary sergeants.

The coup was successful, except for one thing: King Daoud escaped unharmed.

Douglas Mann, the king's bodyguard, had grown suspicious of all of the movement around the king's palace, particularly the presence of so many of Zahim's freshly arrived "technicians." Mann immediately launched a disinformation campaign about the king's schedule, gathered the loyal house guards to his side and then spirited him off the main island to the waiting royal yacht.

An hour after the escape, the blood began to flow.

After Zahim consolidated his position, he had extended an olive branch to the king, guaranteeing his personal safety and offering to pardon him for his crimes against the Kormorellois people.

Hardly the most favorable terms to offer a king, not that any of the loyalists believed the offer.

Even while he was promising reconciliation, General Zahim had a half dozen assassination teams combing the islands for the king.

As HE SAT BACK in the plush limo racing across the island, General Zahim looked like he should be on a college campus somewhere, trolling for coeds.

He had an eager look on his young face, as if he were going out on a date or going to a football game.

But Zahim wasn't going out on a college escapade. Those days were far behind him. The days when he'd attended American universities and a British military academy were far behind him. They were relics of another era.

General Zahim was going off to war again. A war against his people.

He wore an immaculately pressed uniform. The string of medals didn't quite camouflage his youth, but they did distract people's eyes from his baby face.

Not that many people dared to look at him. Too long a gaze, or the "wrong" look could lead to death, or trigger one of his Hitlerian fugues, leading to ranting and raving until either he or his victim collapsed.

General Zahim had never seen live combat, nor had he served with any real army. This coup was his on-the-job training, and without the French military man who mapped out every step he took, he would have been lost.

But he was a fast learner. Especially when it came to killing.

Up ahead he saw Korvois. The capital city of the Kormorelles sprawled uphill in increasing splendor. The poorer and smaller wooden houses on the bottom strip slowly gave way to the grander and elaborate villas on the hill.

Capping the hill was an old white church, one of the island's best-known landmarks. Its steeple had become the transmitter tower of the island's only radio station, giving onlookers the strange impression that it was in direct contact with God.

But the church was a leftover from the colonial days. Its function was to be a spiritual stopover, an unattended chapel kept mainly for the tourists. The rest of the church complex had been turned into shrines to the island gods.

Although General Zahim's attitude toward religion was supposedly one of benign tolerance, he was actually more pragmatic. Zahim felt that as long as the islanders had their gods to turn to in time of trouble, they wouldn't turn against him.

And so while he left his people to pursue their religion, it wasn't the voice of gods or spirits that preached to the islanders. It was the voice of General Zahim.

His weekly addresses had brought a bit of purgatory to the islands.

Like most insecure leaders, he laced his addresses with endless self-important diatribes about the need for change, change that only a great man could bring about. A man whose selfless example would lead the way.

Zahim authored most of these addresses himself, although now and then he inserted key bits of propaganda that the Frenchman sent his way.

In the old days, the radio station had carried the voice of King Daoud. Rather than indulge in speeches or political tirades, Daoud's weekly broadcasts had been devoted to folktales of the island. Music and poetry were regularly featured.

Daoud was intent on showing his people the human side of the king. In line with that, he made himself easily accessible, and he kept his residence opposite the church open to the populace.

Literally the only thing separating church and state was the cobblestoned road.

Daoud was a fool, Zahim thought as his entourage sped along the road. The people should only appear in the palace when they were summoned.

The residence was made predominantly of white-washed stone and had an arched entrance. Inside the courtyard it was possible to see a parade of stone columns supporting splendid walkways and balconies.

The palatial grounds almost had the dignified air of an Ivy League college, with several graceful statues positioned like sentries along the way. General Zahim had complemented them with real sentries from the elite guard of the NKA.

From the courtyard a brick Roman arch led into what was formerly known as the petitioner's hall, where any islander could petition the king.

In the days of the king's reign, there were not that many islanders who took advantage of the king's availability. They seldom bothered him with minor concerns. But if it was a real problem that merited the king's attention, he would unstintingly give it.

These days the petitioner's hall had been turned into official quarters for a tribunal to which no one ever came voluntarily.

Rather they were brought here for some real or imagined offense against the general or his policies. Here their fate would be decided. It was more of an interrogation session than a council. Many of the accused men were given a chance to atone for their crimes by joining the ranks of the NKA. And often attractive women were invited to join the ranks of the general's bedmates.

That was one trait he shared with the king. Though he publicly belittled Daoud for his harem, Zahim exceeded anything the king had done. Yet the king's women had stayed with him voluntarily. The general dragooned women into his life, and ordered them around like slaves. He considered privileges like that to be the perks of leadership. After all, a man of great powers and responsibility was entitled to extraordinary hungers, he thought with satisfaction as he noted their arrival.

He stepped out of the white limousine and paused to run his hand over the smooth and gleaming rooftop. It shone like a beacon beneath the hot afternoon sun, a brilliant reflection of the glory he would bring to the island nation.

The limo met his approval, and not only for the luxury it offered him. It was a gift donated by the main resort complex in the Kormorelles—after he had mentioned in a conversation with the hotelier how suitable it would be for the leader of the new republic.

Zahim glanced downhill at the rainbow-colored houses that flanked the wide cobblestoned road.

Some of them were whitewashed stone, others were painted bright tropical colors. More were of soft pastels. In the dazzling sun, they looked charming and quaint.

Surrounded by his retinue of advisers who pulled up in smaller vehicles, Zahim approached the former presidential palace that had become his quarters. Just as he reached the top step that led to the entrance, he heard a loud whining sound, followed by a screech of brakes.

He frowned, looking at the tanned French mercenary who hopped out of his jeep. It was parked almost parallel to the general's limo.

The man was presumptuous, not only in this act, but in many ways.

Two more jeeps screeched to a halt behind the first one. The Frenchman's lieutenants stayed inside.

Zahim tried to dismiss the affront. There was nothing else he could do. For now. Without Simon Dargient he was a military dictator without any military know-how.

What galled him the most was Dargient's refusal to act like a subordinate. The Frenchman also refused to show any fear. What could he do with a man like that? Zahim wondered for a moment.

But the answer came immediately.

He could rule a country with a man like that. Dargient had engineered the coup every step of the way.

Now his task was to help Zahim cement the takeover and to assist in drawing up blueprints for the future of the island empire.

Dargient pushed through the line of guards at the bottom of the steps, then hurried up to the general's side.

Even though Dargient was standing one step lower than the general, Zahim still had to look up to him.

Simon Dargient was everything the general was not. He was tall and broad-shouldered and always ready to laugh at himself or others, revealing a wide smile that looked incongruous because of a thin scar that bisected the left side of his mouth and chin. Sometimes when he smiled in anger, the translucent scar tissue looked almost like a fang.

Dargient reminded Zahim of one of those Heidelberg princelings who considered a dueling scar of more import than their degrees.

But of course the scar didn't come from a duel. At least not a friendly one.

Zahim himself had asked Dargient where he obtained the scar, and the Frenchman immediately replied in that mocking way of his and patted the long knife he kept sheathed in his belt. "Why? Would you like one, *mon général*?"

"Just curious, Simon," Zahim had responded.

"It came from my work," Dargient said. "More than that you need not know."

The man was insufferable, but also irreplaceable.

You'd never know by looking at him that Dargient had been a military man for the past twenty years— ever since his teens. He wore his black hair slightly long in the front so that it hung boyishly down his forehead, the style giving him a scruffy and almost careless manner that belied his precise and often brutal tactics. He looked more like someone who preferred lounging around the beach, instead of assaulting one. But he was the best that money could buy.

However, when Zahim had negotiated a contract with him, one of those traditional sayings came to his mind. *Let the buyer beware.*

"General Zahim," Dargient said, folding his arms casually in front of him. "We've got to talk."

"Simon," Zahim replied, nodding as if giving the man permission to speak after the fact. "And what is so urgent?"

"There's a problem with the Tanzanians."

General Zahim sighed. He looked at the shaded interior of the presidential palace. The courtyard beckoned invitingly. Subjects awaited him there. Men and women both, whose fate lay in his hands.

"Can it wait?"

Simon shook his head. "No," he said. "Not really. Jean Blanc needs some instruction. I'll take care of it. I just wanted you to know beforehand that it could be expensive."

"With you it is always expensive," Zahim said.

"Revolutions don't come cheap," he said. "Popular or otherwise."

It occurred to Zahim that he'd better discuss things in greater detail with the mercenary, but he knew already that the Frenchman would convince him of anything he wanted.

"You have my blessing."

Simon nodded, smiled as if he'd just received the okay to cuckold the general, then turned and hurried back down the steps.

General Zahim strolled through the arches.

He was in full uniform, his clothes crisp and clean, his medals and Sam Browne holster proudly on display.

As Zahim walked into the room, his fingers danced across the back of his pistol grip as if he were entertaining the idea of shooting down anyone who didn't show the proper respect.

His private bodyguards followed closely, fanning out behind him, their hands also perilously close to their weapons.

He walked down the gauntlet of nervous dignitaries he'd summoned to the palace. They'd been waiting for two hours, standing at attention.

A number of them were minor officials. Others belonged to the royal entourage, men who had kept the king's coffers filled and the machinery of government running smoothly.

Unlike the cabinet ministers who were confined to another area of the palace, these men and women were given their freedom. But they were not so free that they could resist a summons, nor say what they actually thought.

Since he still had not issued a proclamation about what his permanent title would be, they addressed him with various terms designed to show respect for his position.

"Excellency..."

"Mr. President..."

"General..."

"An honor to obtain this audience with you..."

Some of them bowed as they spoke, more out of fear of meeting his eyes than following protocol.

In the first days of the coup, General Zahim had been known to shoot "traitors" on the spot. The fact that they were traitors was known only to him. It was almost a matter of instinct, somewhat like divine deduction.

No doubt there were some among the people he had summarily executed who had sincerely wished him dead, and may have actually been plotting against him. And though the rest of the "traitors" may have wished him dead, they certainly wouldn't have made a move against him.

That didn't matter.

Zahim had to create examples. He had to be obeyed without any pause for thought. The islanders had to consider it a matter of self-preservation to carry out his every whim. Or face the consequences.

Zahim had followed Dargient's instructions in that regard. He'd been careful to execute no foreigners. It was important that none of the tourists were intimidated. If the island's revenues were to be maintained, the outsiders had to feel safe.

There was no doubt that wealthy tourists would continue to visit the Kormorelles. As Dargient had explained, tourists had no qualms about vacationing in a country ruled by dictatorship as long as the linen was clean and room service wasn't interrupted.

Even while the coup had been in effect, Dargient had detailed a well-trained force of mercenaries to safeguard the tourists, assisting them back to their hotels, which were far away from the violence.

To prevent any outside government from invading the Kormorelles to rescue their citizens, General Zahim had offered immediate evacuation from the island to all foreign nationals. And though the leadership had changed, the island ambience was quickly restored. But that was a surface impression only, and as long as Dargient was there to work behind the scenes, no tourists would have the ability to scratch beneath the surface.

General Zahim sat on his "throne," a wooden chair that had been stripped of its lush upholstery and ornate posts. It was now simply a seat of power, stripped-down and raw.

He glanced at the people he'd summoned for the day's business. They formed two lines. They were trembling.

Beautiful, Zahim thought. It was working just as Dargient had said. They would outdo themselves to serve him, and they would gladly turn in suspected conspirators to stay in his good graces.

Zahim let his eyes rove over the line, going from face to face, savoring the fear he found and identifying those who could not hide the anger burning in their eyes.

Finally he settled on his first course of terror and humiliation.

"Mr. Bouillon," he said.

The wealthy pear-shaped landowner waddled forward with apparent reluctance. Of the belief that being overweight marked him as a man of means, Bouillon was one of the island's notable society folk.

"Yes, General," Bouillon said, remembering that he had once made remarks about Zahim being an ill-educated lout despite his extensive toils in the halls of academe.

Zahim ignored him. Instead he turned to the slender and dark-eyed woman who'd been standing beside Bouillon, a native beauty who had succumbed to Bouillon's wealth and position.

"And Mrs. Bouillon," Zahim said.

She stepped forward to take her place beside her husband.

"Yes?" she said, recognizing that it was the one single word that Zahim liked to hear.

"I would like to see you after this audience is finished."

Her husband stood there immobile.

"May I ask for what?" she said.

Zahim bowed his head slightly, his leering eyes telling her the real tale as he said, "Why, to *talk*, of course."

"We'd be delighted to stay," Bouillon said.

The general glared at him. "No, Mr. Bouillon. Just her. You will have an escort home. While she stays here...and talks..."

The general lifted his arm in a dismissive wave that made the couple step back and take their place in the audience line.

He resumed glaring at the assembly, making them quiver while he decided upon whom he would next practice the politics of terror.

4

The speedboat knifed across the stretch of open water that separated Ducroix Island from the western coast of Grand Kormorelle Island.

Simon Dargient guided the high-speed powerboat between the weathered rock icons that guarded the bay. Shaped like crosses, the dolmens were engraved with ornate carvings from ancient islanders, as well as the French pirates who'd settled on Ducroix.

Graffitti of the gods, Dargient thought.

Because of the cross-shaped monuments, the French pirates had originally named the island Deux Croix, which had been bastardized over the years into Ducroix.

And once again it was home to pirates.

But these were a new breed, a more legitimate type of pirates. At the core were the mercenary outfits that Dargient had imported from a half-dozen countries to conduct General Zahim's revolution.

Dargient spun the wheel at the last possible moment to bring the boat in sideways, swamping the rickety dock with a spray of water.

He hopped out of the boat, leaving his chief aides, Corporal Gautier and Gerard Montfort to tie up while he headed straight for one of the makeshift barracks that sat on the edge of a slope facing the ocean.

The barracks had a dusty and sleepy atmosphere, as if the entire camp was knocked out of commission by the blistering sun overhead.

"Blanc!" he shouted, ten yards from the door of the barracks. "Out here. Now!"

Jean Blanc, the tall Tanzanian mercenary, staggered out of the barracks a moment later. He looked fogged, perhaps from the notorious binge he and his crew had been on for the past few days, commandeering a couple of fishing boats to get to one of the resort hotels.

Blanc snapped to attention, his crisp salute contrasting with the rumpled and torn clothes in which he'd collapsed into his bunk.

"You and I must talk," Dargient said.

"Yes, Captain Dargient."

Dargient glared impassively at the Tanzanian. Then he looked at the faces that peered out of the barracks. Some were Blanc's men, but there were also members of the other troops.

Dargient liked Blanc in a way. He followed orders well. Sometimes exceeded them. But there was a matter of discipline.

Blanc's punitive raid against the islanders had gone off perfectly. But it was after the raid that Blanc, or more correctly, Blanc's crew, had created problems.

"Assemble your men tonight," he said. "Everyone who was on the raid. We will celebrate the occasion."

"Thank you, Captain, but that is not necessary," Blanc said, eager to avoid any contact with the Frenchman. "We have already...gone to town."

"So I've heard, Jean Blanc. So I've heard." He glanced at the other mercenaries. "It appears that you all had quite a time."

"The men blew off some steam."

"And shot off their mouths a bit too much," Dargient added.

Blanc nodded in agreement, deciding direct opposition wouldn't be successful. "I must agree with you," he said as calmly as possible.

"That is why we have everything we need on this island," Dargient said. "Barracks and bordello. Bars. Food. You can feast, fight, or screw until daylight all right here on this island."

A lot of thought had been given to the design of the Ducroix camps on the island. Most of them were spread out like spokes in a wheel. And dead in the center, the axle upon which they spun, was the bordello.

Dargient had flown in a contingent of prostitutes to complement the locals. Enough to keep the army satisfied.

There was no reason to go off the island for kicks.

"Tonight at 2200 hours," Dargient said. "Have your people ready."

"Yes, Captain," Blanc said.

Dargient nodded. "Dismissed," he said.

Blanc saluted the Frenchman, spun around and then headed back to the barracks considerably more sober than when he'd tumbled out.

There was going to be some severe punishment handed out. Guard duty. Conditioning. Confinement. All the possibilities ran through Blanc's mind. But by the time he reached the barracks he was reconciled to it.

He thought of the broads and the brawls from last night. It was all still fresh in his mind, playing over and over in his head like a collection of greatest hits.

He shrugged.

It came with the territory. Territory he and his men had occupied time and time again in the past.

They'd had their fun, now they had to pay the piper.

A CONVOY OF BEAT-UP JEEPS, island taxis and Range Rovers roared into the barracks, their headlights cutting through the night as they splayed over the buildings.

Jean Blanc stood in front of his men as one of the jeeps bore straight down on him.

Dargient screeched on the brakes at the last possible moment, the bumper just barely nudging the Tanzanian mercenary's knees as the vehicle came to a halt.

Dargient slammed the door and sprinted over to the assembled mercs.

"Very good, men," he said. "I'm glad to see you're all here."

His good mood was infectious, wiping away most of the nerves that had been gathering on the mercs. He was dressed in his usual off-duty clothes of jeans and chamois shirt, and his ever-present shoulder holster.

"All right, then," he said. "Are you ready for a night to remember?"

Half a dozen shouts gave him the expected answer.

The mercs had recouped from their binge and were ready to start on another one. Especially if it was part of their orders.

Dargient pointed to Jean Blanc, then selected two other Tanzanians to join him. As soon as they were in the vehicle, Dargient stomped the gas pedal, fishtailing the jeep around in a circle, kicking up dust as they headed toward the bordello road.

Dargient drove straight down the middle of the road, heading flat out for a bar full of bad women and good drink.

The man sitting to his right narrowed his eyes, watching the white-lined road devoured by the jeep. Slim, and his beard freshly trimmed, the mercenary looked ready for a night on the town.

Jean Blanc and another Tanzanian merc sat in the back of the roofless jeep. The man beside Blanc was trying to smoke a cigarette, but the speed of the jeep sent a constant airstream into the back seat, blowing embers and smoke all around his face.

Dargient zipped through a phalanx of trees where a section of jungle closed in on the road, then accelerated even more when they came to a long straightaway that cut through the sand dunes.

Halfway down the straightaway, Dargient pulled over to the side of the main road, then sped down a dirt road that ended in a huge parking lot. Loud music blared from several of the bars and bordellos, accompanied by raucous laughter and snatches of inarticulate conversation.

Most of the structures were little more than extended huts or elaborate lean-tos. Plank walkways led from one building to another, although many of the planks had long ago sunk into the mud from the rains.

Dargient parked at the edge of the dusty clearing, keeping the engine idling as he looked back over his shoulder at the headlights approaching behind him. Half a dozen other vehicles swerved over to the sides, parking slightly to the rear of the lead jeep.

With his left hand on the steering wheel, Dargient turned to his right and said, "I've been thinking."

Blanc, sitting directly behind him, nodded. "What have you been thinking about?" Along with the other mercs, he was keeping one eye on the bars where the entertainment waited, while he half concentrated on what Dargient was about to say.

But Dargient didn't say anything. Instead, with one fluid motion, he drew his Browning Hi-Power automatic and pressed it against the temple of the man on his right.

The Tanzanian merc smiled as if it were some kind of joke, a test that Dargient liked to put his people through. Then Dargient pulled the trigger.

The 9 mm slug rocketed through the man's head, searing through skull and bone in a gray-and-red spray. The impact of the bullet sent him slumping against the door.

Without even wasting a split second, Dargient spun around in his seat, extending the smoking Browning barrel like a magic wand that made both of the Tanzanian mercs shrink back into their seats.

After his menacing attitude removed any idea they may have had of attacking him, he returned his attention to the man in the front seat who was now an almost lifeless husk. Despite it all, he was making some kind of strange sound, the sound of a man suspended between two worlds.

Even while the roar from the first shot was still loud in their ears, Dargient pulled the trigger again. Blood and blast filled the air once more.

The merc nodded as the bullet ripped through him. Then he tumbled forward, just as similar gunshots sounded from the vehicles parked on both sides behind him.

Dargient turned around, resting his gun hand on the back of the seat. "Like I said, I've been thinking about making some changes around here."

Jean Blanc suddenly looked lighter, as if he were trying to levitate out of the seat. The only thing that kept him from making a move was the knowledge that Simon Dargient never wasted any moves. If he meant to kill them all, he would have just drilled them by the roadside, one, two, three.

Dargient spoke conversationally, as if the ghost of the merc in the front seat hadn't just flown soulless into the afterlife.

"Your men have been talking in the wrong bars, Jean," he said.

Blanc nodded slowly.

"You see, here on the island, among their own troops, if the men want to brag about the raids they've made, the terror they've instilled in the natives, that's fine. But when they're sloppy enough to go into a hotel and let the waiters, waitresses and entertainers hear all about their exploits..."

"But, Captain," Blanc said. "You said yourself our mission was to paralyze the islanders—"

"Yes," Dargient said. "But not to talk about it openly when your men are drunk and disorderly in public. Particularly when they are drunk and disorderly in places that are off-limits to them."

The Frenchman paused for a moment, raising his Browning and idly tapping it on the back of his seat. "What shall I do about this lapse of discipline?"

Blanc shrugged nonchalantly, but the man beside him watched Dargient closely. Although the Frenchman was no longer pointing the gun at him, he had no doubt that it could go off at any time. Tonight. Tomorrow. Next week.

"It's all a matter of security," Dargient continued, as though he were merely imparting information. "We launch an operation. It gets done. It stays done. It's not supposed to come undone because someone talks about it. Of course, the people already know that we're behind the death squads..."

For emphasis he gestured with the hand that held the gun, knowing that his audience followed every motion with apprehensive interest.

"But there has to be a deniability," Dargient said. "As a matter of politics, we have to be able to blame the attacks on rebels. On royalists. We must be able to say we don't know anything about it." Dargient shook his head from side to side, pained at having to spell it out to the men. "We can't go around having instant replay from loose lips whenever you feel like it."

Dargient glanced back at the lifeless body. "I think *he* understands me now." Then he looked each man steadily in the eye. "The question is, do you understand me? Or should I—" he raised the Browning "—explain some more?"

"I understand, Captain Dargient," Blanc said, and the same sentiment was immediately echoed by his fellow mercenary.

"Good," Dargient said, breaking into a smile made crooked by his scar as he resumed his cheerful manner. He holstered the Browning. "In a few days, Jean Blanc, you'll be receiving some replacements for the men you've lost tonight. Could you do me a favor and make sure they share in our understanding of discipline?"

"Yes, Captain," Blanc said.

"Very well." Dargient reached into his pocket and withdrew a bundle of rolled up bills. He handed them to Blanc and said, "Now, go and have a good time tonight. On me."

Blanc took the money. Then, as if hypnotized, he and the other mercenary climbed out of the jeep and headed toward the bright lights.

Several other Tanzanians emerged from the vehicles parked behind them, but each group of mercenaries that left the vehicles had one less soldier than when they started out the night.

Simon Dargient drove off, ignoring the silent and dead cargo beside him.

He'd made it a point long ago to let nothing bother him. By now the sight of death had absolutely no effect. It was all in a day's work.

SIMON DARGIENT WAS BACK in his quarters at the presidential palace shortly after midnight, thanks to the island-hopping boats and vehicles always at his command.

He could commandeer tour buses, taxis, military jeeps, yachts, or speedboats, whatever he needed.

There were very few who would argue the point with Dargient. Whatever was available was his for the taking. The island offered many things—most recently a woman named Lalana.

Taller than most of the Kormorellois, she was stretched out on his bed alluringly. She cushioned her head on her arm as she glanced sideways at him, perhaps hoping that she could hold on to him. He'd scooped her up from the hotel bar where she'd been pushing drinks and established her in the safety of the palace where all she had to do was to please him.

She'd been there for several nights running.

Unlike the general, Dargient wasn't interested in quantity. He was interested in quality. And she made sure that the quality of life, especially his nightlife, left nothing to be desired.

Tonight she'd adorned herself with flowers and had worn her luxuriant black hair gathered in braids with tiny glittering seashells hanging from the end. The shells made clinking sounds when she tilted her head coquettishly at him, but Dargient hadn't really noticed.

He'd thrown himself at her roughly and impatiently, and then just as quickly left the bed.

But at least, she mused, he hadn't booted her out after using her, the way many of his kind would have done. Instead he'd just allowed her to become invisible as she lay there.

It didn't particularly bother him to have her around and he would feel the same indifference if she left and went back to her own tiny quarters.

She'd tried to make that little cell her own, filling it with flowers and curtains and perfumes, but never managed to defeat that transitory atmosphere.

As long as she lived there, the pleasures of the palace would be available to her. But the pleasures and comforts weren't for individuals. They were perks that went with the position of a palace mistress—a dangerous vocation.

Lalana closed and opened her eyes several times, watching the hazy image of the mercenary captain through the mosquito netting that formed a canopy over the bed. She watched him quietly until she finally drifted off into a welcome sleep.

Simon Dargient was in khaki shorts and a sleeveless T-shirt, sitting by the white stone wall, his feet propped up on the ledge of a wide oval window.

A cool ocean breeze drifted in and out of the room like the tides, stirring up the warm night air with a clean scent of seaweed.

Dargient was wide-awake. He was looking out the unshuttered window at the stars—*his stars, his sky*. He was thinking that out here in the middle of nowhere, a man who knew what he was doing could be king.

Actually, the title didn't matter. He didn't need to be called a general or a king. Those who were closer to him were aware that Simon Dargient would soon be the real power on the Kormorelles, even while he played straight man to the general.

From past lessons he knew he had to stay low-key. No matter how many strings he pulled in reality, it was best if he stayed invisible to the outside world.

The last time he ruled a country, Dargient's brief reign had attracted the attention of nearly every Intelligence service working on the African continent.

It had been fun while it lasted. And he'd managed to get out with his life. If nothing else, it looked good on his résumé.

As Dargient scanned the jewelled canopy arching above the Indian Ocean, he thought back to the world he'd lost, the Western African United Republic, a splinter of land and lakes with a tiny foothold on the Ivory Coast....

SIMON DARGIENT'S REIGN in West Africa came to an end in the classic manner.

Armies on three borders were prepared to march into the republic and reclaim it from the foreigner who'd held an entire country for ransom with a hand-picked army of outcasts and mercenaries.

Dargient was all set to face the music, and in that half belief in sheer willpower that plagued many a mercenary, had hopes that he would emerge triumphant. But then he received a visit from a former mentor.

The mentor was officially a diplomat, a Frenchman at home in the courts of Europe, the kingdoms of Africa, or behind the trigger of a submachine gun.

His mentor's name was Claude Auxerre, and though he'd left the uniform of the French Foreign Legion behind, he'd never left the training. In fact, the legion was but one of several outposts along the military career of the man who came to deliver an ultimatum to Simon Dargient.

Auxerre and Dargient spoke the same language. It was the language of war, the language of realpolitik. Despite their friendship from the past, there were no illusions between the two, no false hopes to prop up.

At times both Dargient and Auxerre had served as officers in the same regiment in the legion. *Regiment Etranger de Parachutistes.*

They had made the drop into Zaire for the rescue of the predominately white technicians and civilians holed up at Kowlwezi. Together they came under the fire of the Katangese rebels who were acting as if they were on a holiday of slaughter until the legion arrived.

There were other occasions when they also fought in the same countries—but on opposite sides.

Auxerre was still marching for the French government, operating under a number of guises. Whatever his title or affiliation, he carried out the wishes of the covert French forces, in much the same manner as Simon Dargient carried out the wishes of Simon Dargient.

There was a guarded respect between the two men. At the best of times Auxerre used other men, and had thrown Dargient to the wolves when it was necessary. But there were unexpected times when he had tried to help.

Now, as the ruins of the WAUR fell all around Dargient, Auxerre had come to pay his last respects to the government.

"Thank you for agreeing to seeing me," he'd said upon first stepping into Dargient's office.

Auxerre's steel-gray hair was perfectly cut, and his bearing showed the same kind of steel. In his midforties, he followed a regimen that made many a younger man collapse.

"Anytime," Dargient replied. "It is always a pleasure to see an old *friend*."

"Nice location," Auxerre said, clasping his hands behind him as he strolled over to the windows that looked down upon Mkolale Airport.

Dargient smiled. He'd said *nice location*, not *nice office*, though it was paneled and furnished in mahogany, and decked out with gold and silver pieces.

To Auxerre's mind it was a nice location for a headquarters because it was right next to an airport where a plane could be kept in readiness, and it was only a few miles away from the Atlantic in case Dargient's people had to make a run for it.

"I've learned a few things over the years," Dargient admitted.

Auxerre cocked his head. "Yes," he said. "I've noticed. I've been following your exploits in the press...and elsewhere. Although I must admit that you've made it hard from time to time by using so many different names. But whatever name you go by, sooner or later the tracks of the *The Cardinal* always emerge."

"The Cardinal" was a name that had stuck after he had cynically but in some ways quite appropriately chosen "Richelieu" as a nom de guerre while he'd been advising some of the more notorious African despots.

"You taught me well, Claude."

"Too well, it seems."

"*That* depends where you stand," Dargient said.

"From where I stand, it seems just fine."

"From my perspective," Auxerre said, "drastic measures are called for." Coming from Auxerre, that sentiment considerably sobered Dargient.

For several years Claude Auxerre had worked for *Service de Documentation Extérieure et Contre-*

Espionnage, the extremely professional and professionally brutal French Intelligence agency. While working out of the SDECE headquarters on Boulevard Mortier, Auxerre had elicited considerable respect and occasional fear from his counterparts in the Western Intelligence agencies.

Though the agency had since been changed, Auxerre's methods were still quite the same. Thorough and final. And though it was logic, not fear, that brought Dargient up short, the effect was the same. Going against Auxerre was the equivalent of smashing into a brick wall.

Dargient offered Auxerre a cognac. Then, separated only by the wide desk, the two men raised their glasses.

Last drink. Last rites.

They finished their drinks, then dropped into their chairs.

"I've come to kill you, Dargient," the diplomat said.

"Is there time for another drink first?" Dargient said, rising from the desk and walking toward the ornate bar he'd installed shortly after he took the reins of power from the African prince he'd been working for.

Auxerre shrugged. He lightly rubbed his hands together as if he were washing them, then spread them apart.

Dargient returned with another bottle of cognac. He poured them each another glass, then raised his. "To old soldiers," he said.

Auxerre returned the toast. "May they never die," he said, "unnecessarily."

The French diplomat sipped the cognac, then set his glass down on the black leather top of the desk. "I came here against the wishes of my superiors." The way he'd said superiors indicated that he believed no one could ever earn such a title.

"I appreciate that," Dargient said.

"They simply wanted me to come in here, blazing away as if it were some tawdry cowboy operation. Bring in a regiment and take you out. Destroy the building. Destroy the country."

"Now I really appreciate your coming here in this manner," Dargient said. "May I ask why?"

"I told them you were a reasonable man," Auxerre said. "That logic might be the best currency for a man in your position." He paused. "Then there is the matter of logistics. Obtaining the covert approval of WAUR's neighbors. Or perhaps violating their air space for a strike. Also, I had to consider the likelihood that you would escape and I would have to hunt you down. It all had the potential to get very complicated and expensive."

"I see your reasoning," Dargient said, "but I'm driven by more than reason,"

"*Beyond* reason, at times," Auxerre replied.

"Like everyone else, Claude, I am driven by money. I have expenses, debts to pay. Burial bonuses for the men I've lost on this trip. The whole lot."

"Of course," Auxerre said. He smiled broadly. "This is why I told my superiors that we could simply pay your price. Purchase your abdication."

Dargient had thought it over. He had already fulfilled his contract for his French backers. He'd installed the prince, then helped him loot the country's treasury. Afterward, as planned, he'd expelled the prince to a life of luxurious exile. By that time there was little left in the country but a people who were primed to explode.

Now Dargient was offered an out by his former mentor.

He could walk out, or he could be carried out. Perhaps he and the mentor would go out together in a blaze of glory. There was a lot to be said for that, but then he wouldn't be around to hear the tale of the Cardinal, told with a whisper and a laugh.

There could always be another place, another time. And maybe next time it would be the right place.

"It is against my better judgment," Dargient had said, "but out of respect for you, my friend, I could not let your superiors think you misjudged me. I accept your offer."

"D'accord," Auxerre said, pointedly fastening the holster flap over his 9 mm Sig-Sauer double-action automatic. "Now let us get down to real business." He grabbed the neck of the cognac bottle and poured the first of several glasses.

And Simon Dargient left the country. He took with him his small private bodyguard and the considerable sum that Auxerre had negotiated for him. He went underground, spending a lot of time checking out where it was best to surface.

Dargient looked hard to find what he considered the best deal, where he would be unfettered by the chains of government, even the almost friendly chains wielded by men like Auxerre.

He found the perfect horizon at the Kormorelles, where there was a king in need of dethroning and a general in need of guidance.

Here he could be a secret king and wield major power.

It was a daring move, but he wasn't totally alone. He had the right people in his own bodyguard to help him carry it off. And he had the right stuff. The first step in becoming a king, even an unacknowledged king, was to live like one.

Dargient pushed his feet off the window ledge, the legs of the tilted chair coming down hard with a *whack* that awoke Lalana.

She stirred at his approach and then smiled up at him through the haze of sleep.

Dargient moved in beside her, and soon he was sleeping the fearless sleep of a creature of prey.

5

Nile Barrabas unrolled a map of the Kormorelles and spread it across the table in the main salon of the yacht. The salon had been converted into a war room, and though it was still plush, the atmosphere in the room was strictly business.

Barrabas had set up charts on the wall showing various locales of the islands, the layouts of the presidential palace and the island barracks with their approximate troop strengths.

He blew a stream of cigar smoke across the maps, for a moment making the islands appear as if they were clouded with a mist of volcanic smoke.

There were six main islands and almost a hundred other small islands, reefs and coral atolls, stretching like the debris of a lost continent across the Indian Ocean. Some of them were little more than spits of sand, others were dense oases of rain forests full of herds of wild pig and the deerlike spiked-horn eland. A good number of the islands were too small to be portrayed on an island map, let alone a larger regional map.

Many of the Kormorelles had finger bays and coves where powerboats could easily lay hidden. Although there was considerably less shelter for vessels the size of the royal yacht, there were still a number of safe harbors for the king's ship, like the one in which the yacht was anchored.

It was a narrow strait that wound through two walls of volcanic rock, treacherous waters except for those who knew it intimately.

Fortunately Douglas Mann, Daoud's British bodyguard and adviser, had foreseen the need to keep the harbors uncharted, making sure they were unmarked on the maps that were available to the Kormorelles.

Barrabas tapped his finger on the portion of the map that showed the Bay of Glass on Mirror Island, just south of Grand Komorelle.

Most of the resort buildings ringed the Bay of Glass, their luxury suites and balconies facing the calm mirrorlike waters that gave the tourists the impression of wading into a picture postcard.

The rest of the place reinforced the fairy-tale quality. Silvery pools and ribbons of streams crisscrossed the island, giving it an enchanting and almost otherworldly atmosphere.

"How easy is it for troops to move from Grand Kormorelle across the Bay of Glass?"

Mann shrugged. "As easy as putting one foot in front of the other," he said. "Actually there's a couple of ways. First there's the quarter-mile bridge, which connects Grand Kormorelle to Mirror. It's open most of the time and brings you right to Glass Boulevard, which runs through the developed sector of the island.''

Barrabas nodded.

''Then there's the second way. With speedboats and fishing boats they could transport their men and supplies without too much trouble. There are a number of troublesome reefs, but someone familiar with the waters can easily pilot their way in.''

''Nothing we can't fix,'' Barrabas said. ''If we have to.'' Barrabas then turned his attention back to Grand Kormorelle.

The main island of Grand Kormorelle was totally under the control of the NKA. From the presidential palace down to the streets, there was a strong presence of mercenaries, militia and policemen who'd acted as a combination palace guard and goon squad.

Since the coup, General Zahim had imported several new contingents of mercenaries. That was Zahim's strength and weakness combined into one. The mercenaries were composed of predominantly African and French troops. Many of the African contingents had long simmering feuds that carried over from the continent, and thus had to be kept away from one another.

Barrabas would bring them together soon, when the SOBs visited the island.

The majority of Zahim's troops were spread out on Grand Kormorelle and nearby Ducroix Island where there were several barracks. The SOB chief knew where the main strengths of the enemy lay. Now he had to find out where the allies of the king—or president—were the strongest.

Mann gave him a rundown of so-called safehouses and arms caches.

Most of the king's potential backers were on Mirror Island, while the foot soldiers were on Grand Kormorelle. Both were equally important and had to be won over to the cause.

Naturally the entrepreneurs who'd brought in the money to develop the islands preferred to deal with a more stable personality than a power-mad general. But realistically they would deal with whoever held the reins of power. They would play both sides until a clear victor emerged.

But there was one thing that Barrabas was sure of: they would play the game. The money-makers weren't babes in the woods. If they saw a chance to return to the more peaceful days of Daoud's rule, they would take it.

It was up to Barrabas to present them with that chance, and to accomplish that, he had to learn as much about the opposition and his allies as possible.

After further conferring with Mann, Barrabas sought another consultation with the king.

Daoud entered the salon, and inspected the maps that possibly had indications of his personal future. Barrabas had made several markings on them—troop strengths, sights for raids, escapes, safehouses, ideal observation points, choke holds.

"I see you are preparing to go to work," Daoud said. His gaze swept around the salon, as if seeking reassurance from the air of efficiency and organization.

"Soon," Barrabas said. He rolled up some of the maps and pushed them to one side of the table, making room for Daoud to sit at the table. "First I would like to make a few things perfectly clear about my intentions."

"Whatever you say," Daoud said.

"Don't be so quick to agree," Barrabas said. "You're not going to like what I have to say."

Daoud raised his hand. "Nonetheless, I am sure you have your reasons."

"I do," Barrabas said. "First—" he spread his hand to take in the salon and the yacht "—how much did this run to?"

"The yacht?"

"Yes."

Daoud shrugged. "The original price was in the millions," he said. "I don't have the figures at hand. Then there were the renovations, modifications. All in all, it's a very handsome price."

"I'm sure it is," Barrabas said.

"Why do you ask, Mr. Barrabas?"

Barrabas met the king's eyes and said, "I want you to realize what you're giving up when I sink it."

"Sink it?" the king said.

"It appears it might have to be that way. The yacht's too large to hide forever—and yes, Douglas told me all about the hidden cave you have prepared for it. But this is like painting a target on the middle of your forehead and wondering why everyone's shooting at you.''

"The expense..." Daoud said.

"More expensive to keep it," Barrabas said. "But don't worry. We'll salvage what we can. Particularly the Nightfox."

The helipad on the rear deck had room for the Nightfox, which Douglas Mann and two native Kormorellois were qualified to fly.

The high-tech helo was the king's security blanket, suitable for a quick getaway or an attack. It had state of the art surveillance gear as well as topflight weaponry.

Apparently considering the loss of the yacht to be painful but necessary, Daoud seemed to accept it. "What else do you have in mind?"

To emphasize his words, Barrabas lifted his right hand, chopping the air in front of him. "First we're going to stage a raid to make our presence known and let the royalists realize that Zahim's rule isn't absolute. Before we do that we have to touch base with some of your friends on the islands—and see if they are willing to be supportive."

Now Daoud's attention was fully engaged and Barrabas shot his other hand forward, steepling it against his right hand as if he were preparing to pray. "And then we're going to raise the dead."

Daoud smiled. "Perhaps you really can work miracles," he said.

Barrabas explained a bit about raising the dead. From his previous discussions about the warrior cult, he'd learned of their concept of "the returned ones," who were departed island warriors who bridged the gap between the living and the dead.

The Great Return was at hand.

Barrabas purposely kept his plans vague when speaking to Daoud. He didn't want the king's interference, but he wanted his input. Particularly when it came to the king's half brother. Barrabas wanted to anticipate how he would react in certain circumstances, based on his actions and methods in the past.

The king recounted how Zahim had insinuated himself into positions of control on the island, amassing wealth and gradually sharing in many of Daoud's decisions.

It was Zahim who pressed for the enlargement and modernization of the airport, as well as for an auxiliary airstrip to be built on Ducroix Island, supposedly for the expected influx of cargo and engineering equipment. It had come in handy for Zahim's mercenaries.

There were several other advantages Zahim had lobbied for, always hitting the king for more money, which in the interest of peace, or appeasement, Daoud had provided. In hindsight it was obvious that Zahim was laying the groundwork for his "technicians" to waltz right in and launch their coup.

"That was a problem, giving him so much power," Barrabas said.

"I tried to keep him appeased, and on my side. I had my doubts about him, but I couldn't act. There was no direct proof. Also, he was family, then. Part of our philosophy involves a certain responsibility to those around us. It is our duty to bring them back into the fold.''

"Until they try to kill you," Barrabas said.

"Yes," Daoud agreed. "Once he turned against me and my people, I could renounce him. He is no longer part of my family.''

"And so now you can actively do something against him. You are relieved of responsibility for him. Very practical. I like that in a religion.''

Daoud nodded his head. He looked tired. Drained. "Yes, now we can do whatever is needed. He has joined the other side.''

"The NKA," Barrabas agreed.

"No," Daoud said solemnly, surprising the mercenary leader. "The side of the serpent.''

It was odd, Barrabas thought. Though the king had certainly enjoyed his role as a playboy, there was a fire in his eyes—a religious fervor that hadn't been noticeable before.

"Okay," Barrabas said. "I was never much for holy wars—except as a way to manipulate the other side. You and your priests can fight the serpents. The SOBs will fight the New Kormorelles Army.''

Since he'd first talked to Barrabas, the king's mood had swung from one of mild skepticism to optimism. But at the moment he had no way of knowing which emotion to bank on. Now, seeing that the SOBs were preparing their assault, he had come to accept their way of thinking, which meant that instead of wondering how such odds could be faced, a decision was made to go for it. You went ahead and got it done.

It was a contagious feeling.

The king could see that Barrabas knew what he was doing by asking all the right questions, digesting the answers, and then assuming command. If the countercoup was to be successful, it would be on Barrabas's terms.

"Will you require anything else from me?" Daoud said and started to rise.

"As a matter of fact, yes," Barrabas said. "There is one more front we'll be fighting on."

"What's that?"

"We're going into the hotel business. I'll want an introduction to the main hotelier on Mirror Island."

"Why?" Daoud said.

"So we can enlist him in our army. He will be one of our most valued soldiers, whether he knows it or not."

"It will be done," Daoud said. Then he left the salon.

Douglas Mann, who'd been leafing through an old magazine while he waited patiently for either the king or Barrabas, tossed the magazine on the couch he'd been sitting on. He stood and approached the table.

"Is there anything else you'll be needing?"

Barrabas had already taken out the dossier on Simon Dargient and spread the folder out on the table. From a glossy photograph, the French mercenary stared back at Barrabas with a half smile on his face.

He'd seen the face before in numerous Intelligence reports, customs offices and hanging on walls of run-down police stations.

He too had fought in Africa. He too had toppled rulers, large and small. But Barrabas had never gone against Dargient directly, though he'd wanted to. There had never been the chance, or the need.

"A bit of luck is what I need," Barrabas said. "All you've got." He drew a circle around Dargient's face with the thick black marker he'd previously used on the maps.

Then he drew a cross hairs upon it.

It would take an element of luck to get the French merc in his sights.

And it would take more upheavals. He thought of the once-peaceful islanders he was about to awake. Many of them would die, but then already many of them had suffered innocently. At least Barrabas was going to give them a fighting chance.

Only now, before the battle, could it weigh on his conscience. For him, it was a way of life. For those unused to war, it would be hell. Once it was under way, there would no time for such concerns. It would be a matter of strength, of logistics, of wins and losses.

It was hard to set into motion a chain of events that would cause so much hardship to virtual strangers. To islanders who deserved much better. But there was one thing that helped him in his decision to ignite the fires under the cauldron of war.

Unless he made his move, the terror and crippled life would continue, causing even greater suffering.

For some it would be physical, and for others it would be mental or spiritual.

There was no other way, no other path Barrabas could follow. Death was his province and he'd come to establish dominion.

6

The death squad announced their arrival in customary fashion. As they moved through the forest, they smashed empty bottles against the palm trees. The bursting glass tinkled, sounding like church bells before a ceremony. They were almost upon the village, where dying camp fires cast flickering shadows across the reed-and-thatch walls of the huts. They held their automatic rifles carelessly, like divining rods in search of blood instead of water.

Tonight there were more soldiers than usual. They were thirty strong.

The size of the squad depended on the village and what kind of resistance was expected. So far that hadn't actually happened. Resistance had been an idle fear, and except for a few suicidal gestures, none of the islanders had stood up to the terror.

Still, the death squads weren't prepared to take any risks. No matter what the population of the villages was, they always came in strong enough to squash any opposition.

Tonight's target was a village one mile into the interior of White Ridge Island, whose southern shore was guarded by a series of weathered white cliffs that were often covered in mist.

Although it was far from being a capital, the village of Saralam was a center of tribal life for the islanders. Their herds of pigs and goats and their large well-cultivated plots lent the village a sense of permanence and stability lacking in many other villages.

It was a stability that was about to be tested.

Jean Blanc signaled his men to stop at the edge of the grove. They spread out in a long irregular line, another midnight hunting party about to beat the bush for their prey.

Blanc and his handpicked Tanzanians formed the nucleus of the squad. And while some of the soldiers moved like veterans, others seemed to be wound-up puppets, ready to jump the gun. Newly arrived from Africa, they were Blanc's replacements, and it was their first night on the prowl.

Blanc's terror teams had been moving from one village to the next, island by island, in a predictable pattern. Each attack collected a harvest of victims.

The mercenaries talked about the raids among themselves and enjoyed bending the ears of the newcomers with all the gory details of their raids.

So far these battles had been strictly one-sided. The new recruits in the NKA's night teams had heard the tales of women who were ripe for the taking, of natives who went running for their lives across the beach, splashing into the ocean and bobbing up and down while the mercs shot them for target practice.

But none of the regulars even thought about mouthing off about their activities outside their closely knit circle of terrorists.

Ever since Captain Dargient had given him a lesson about discipline, Jean Blanc worked to forge his men into a more cohesive unit. He'd drilled them constantly and got them used to following orders instantly, looking to him for direction.

But there was still a certain freedom to it. Once the "action" began, he could let them have their own way. The new men would instinctively know what to do.

Shrouded in the grove, on the verge of cutting loose his savages, Jean Blanc felt a sudden rush of excitement in his chest. His heart beat faster. The war was about to begin again.

He savored it, holding on to the moment when he was a predator, when he held the fate of the villagers in his hands—hands that would soon be awash in blood. There was no real fear of combat. What he felt was exhilaration.

Jean Blanc held his M-16 in his left hand and slowly raised his right hand, about to give the command to move forward. Something undefinable alerted him, and he started to swing his M-16 to the right. Then a thin line appeared on his neck, and an invisible force seemed to hold him.

Then the thin line deepened and darkened, becoming liquid. It was a permanent bloody necklace.

Jean Blanc's eyes blurred as he tried to focus on the dizzying horizon in front of him. But he tilted steadily backward, the clarity of his thoughts cut off just as irreversibly as the garrote that had sliced through his neck.

The razor sharp loop had come from behind, wielded by a man who had come too close by the time his presence was sensed.

Nile Barrabas had joined the hunt.

After a strangled hiss of air and a cascade of blood, the Tanzanian mercenary thumped to the ground, never able to give the command to attack.

The man to his right turned and saw a black shadow that was one with the night. He sensed rather than saw the foot flying through the air toward his jaw.

Barrabas's upper body was angled low to the ground as his right foot snapped out. It struck Blanc's man in the side of the head, caving in the column of bone alongside his eye and sending splinters into his brain.

As the Tanzanian's body crumpled to the ground, Barrabas moved on to the others in his arc of attack.

Five other SOBs were clearing out their assigned sectors of the woods, moving silently, tearing into the death squad with a suddenness that made any defensive moves ineffective.

Wearing night-black balaclavas, the only sign of the SOBs presence was the glistening of their eyes, eyes that sized up the situation for a plan of attack that was formulated in seconds, courtesy of their skill and experience.

They struck with knifes, fists, kicks and neck-breaking embraces, and by the time the death squad knew it was engaged in a genuine battle, nearly half of them were on the ground.

A massive-chested Tanzanian looked at the shadows moving around him. He couldn't distinguish friend from foe. All he saw was movement, and the only thing he could think of was to shoot his way through.

As he raised his M-16 to hip level, a circular red light appeared on his forehead. *Thwook.* A needle-sharp bolt sluiced right into the spot where the laser light had been.

The crossbow bolt cracked through his temple, then ripped through the back of his skull. It jerked his head backward as if he were having second thoughts. Then he had no thoughts left as the M-16 dropped to the ground unfired, followed by his lifeless body.

Billy Two moved through the underbrush, locking another bolt into place and then taking aim on another mercenary on the prowl.

He didn't really need the LS 45 Lasersight to locate the enemy. He was using it more for effect than to improve his accuracy. The Osage guerrilla fighter was totally in his element in dark combat. The laser light was a psychological weapon, a demonic light from above. Seeing a light, then seeing the effects of a thunderbolt as it crashed into that spot where the light had been, put the fear of gods into the survivors.

Automatic fire ripped through the night as the surviving members of the death squad opened up. But it didn't last long. Once they started firing, the SOBs poured lead into them from their own silenced submachine guns, the 9 mm slugs ripping through them like chattering metal teeth.

It was no contest.

The SOB's had been tracking the death squad ever since it landed on the island, and as expected, had headed for the next village on the list.

Jean Blanc's tactics and his schedule were well-known.

The royalists they'd contacted through Douglas Mann had clued in the SOBs on what had been happening and Blanc's role in the terror.

The squad had arrived almost on schedule, their favorite time of midnight.

But now *their* time had run out.

Jean Blanc's remaining men looked toward the highest-ranking NKA soldier left alive, ready to follow his lead.

The man ran. He ran screaming, weaponless and mindless, carried away by his own panic.

The SOBs let a surviving handful of NKA hit men escape through the rain forest, carrying with them the ghoulish memory of the creatures of the night.

SOMEHOW THE BODIES of the slain NKA men moved during the night.

A trail of footprints led from the forest where they'd died to an overhang of rock where they were left in a supine position, their arms spread wide in winglike fashion as if they were praying to the gods of the islands and asking for forgiveness.

Rumors spread from the island that it was the work of "the returned ones," the spirits of the warrior ancestors who'd come back to life to seek vengeance on the death squad.

Then, it was widely whispered, those spirits had animated the NKA corpses and walked them to the cliffs.

The returned ones had also led away the villagers of Saralam, taking them to a place where they would be safe.

The word spread quickly, from village to village—and from barracks to barracks as the newly christened NKA men described the phantoms who'd hunted them down in the night.

Apparently the villagers believed in the phantoms enough to place their lives with them. They escaped retribution. When a well-armed team of NKA troops arrived at the village, they found only deserted huts and pens.

And the footprints of corpses.

7

Winding streams tinkled through the hotel grounds. White stone bridges crossed over them, linking the lush green patches of sculpted lawn and hedges that made it look like a private park.

The streams almost looked as if they were designed by nature rather than man.

The architect of The Island Hotel had spent a small fortune to execute his design for the curved coral-lined streambeds that circled like a moat around three-quarters of the complex.

Palms flourished at regular intervals along the streams. There were swimming pools and fountains and white-winged statues perched on marbleized pillars, looking down with sightless and benevolent gazes on the tourists.

Above it all were the pastel-colored towers of The Island, a cathedral dedicated to unabashed luxury.

It was called The Island for two reasons. First there was the actual shape of the complex, which resembled an island with the streams on three sides and a curved beach on the other.

But another reason for the choice of name was a marketing angle. The owners wanted tourists to think of The Island as *the* place to go, synonymous with the lush Garden of Eden setting that the Kormorelles offered. Though there were a number of other hotels flanking it, it was the ultimate retreat on Mirror Island.

Because of its reputation for offering such luxuriant excess, The Island attracted a steady flow of well-heeled tourists.

It also attracted a man with a shock of almost white hair but fit and tanned features, who strolled into the top-floor office of the hotelier.

The hotelier was a man in his fifties who still appeared to have mostly kept middle age at bay, even if he was a little heavy. The tailoring of his suit concealed the slight bulge at the waistline, evidence that he frequently sampled the hotel's esteemed cuisine.

He stepped into his outer office, welcoming his guest even before his receptionist buzzed him. Though he had a broad smile on his face, he kept his eye on the door that led to the elevator—as if he expected someone to storm through it at any moment.

"Mr. Barrabas?" he said.

Nile Barrabas nodded and extended his hand. "And you're William Winthrop."

As they shook hands, Barrabas was surprised to notice the man had a calloused hand and a firm grip, the strength of someone who worked at staying in shape.

With a wave of his arm Winthrop ushered Barrabas into a much larger room. Almost as if it were in keeping with the hotel's main theme, Winthrop's desk gave the impression of being anchored in the center of the room, an island of teak flanked by thin but delicately curved chairs. A curved section of window looked out like a visor upon the Bay of Glass.

Barrabas sat in the chair facing the desk, resting his elbows on the padded arm of the chair. He looked around appreciatively, then remarked, "Things are pretty nice up here at the top of the totem pole."

Winthrop nodded. "It's not bad, and it's part of our public relations effort," he said. "But I'm sure you didn't come here just to tell me that."

The hotelier was edgy, like a man who was in the middle and sitting across from somebody who was about to give another turn to the vise.

"I'm here on behalf of the king," Barrabas said.

"Yes," Winthrop said. "So I gather." He had received a call from King Daoud informing him that Barrabas was coming, and that he was a man who had to be seen.

From his evasive look, Winthrop apparently hoped he could leave it at that. He would see Barrabas quickly, but he would be more eager to see him go.

But Barrabas showed no sign that it was a courtesy visit. Evidently he was prepared to stay until it suited him to leave.

Winthrop knew the kind of setup they wanted him to be party to. He had been involved in a number of deals where there was always a man or two behind the scenes, people who called the shots.

Sometimes Winthrop had been in that position. More often than not, he'd been on the other end. A man who listened. A man who carried out orders.

Now he was confronted by a man who looked like he was used to giving orders. Though Barrabas had traded in his combat togs for pinstripes, his bearing marked him as a military man.

"But why did the king send you?" Winthrop asked.

"There are a lot of answers to that," Barrabas said. "But I think I can show you quite quickly exactly why I'm here."

"Please do," Winthrop said.

Barrabas shoved himself off his chair and headed for the curved glass. From farther back, a backdrop of clouds and the light blue sky over the Indian Ocean could be seen through the windows. But up close to the glass the scenery changed to a different but no less lovely view.

One of the hotel's pools lay directly below the window. And beyond that was the prime beachfront owned by The Island Hotel.

"Take a look at this," Barrabas said.

Prepared to sit throughout the entire meeting in an effort to maintain a semblance of control, Winthrop frowned. But nevertheless he got up and walked to the window.

"Look down there and tell me what you see," Barrabas instructed.

Winthrop shrugged. He saw what he was used to seeing. A number of blondes sans bikini stretched out on the lounges around the pool. Several couples lolling with their feet in the water. A few kids scouting the grounds for trouble.

Most of them were repeat guests who'd discovered the charms of the Kormorelles, charms that remained stable even through a revolution. Since the revolution had been so quickly contained and confined to the other islands, life went on as usual on the Bay of Glass.

After looking around for a few moments, Winthrop turned to Barrabas and said, "I see my guests doing what they like to do. Having the time of their lives, which they've paid for in advance. Well in advance of the troubles. They pay me to make the world stop for a while, and that's what I do here at The Island."

"Funny," Barrabas said. "We're both looking out the same window, but we're seeing something completely different."

"And what do you see, Mr. Barrabas?" Winthrop said, still holding on to the tone of voice he used to charm his guests.

Barrabas shrugged. "First, don't call me mister. I'm not a guest here. Call me Barrabas or Nile, whichever you prefer. And as for what I see down there—" Barrabas scanned the poolside once more "—I see a group of well-heeled hostages."

Winthrop stepped away from the window, as if he were dismissing a vision. "Impossible," he said. "I've been assured by General Zahim himself that nothing would happen to any of the hotel guests and—"

"But Zahim isn't really calling the shots. He's not smart enough to pull this off."

"Yes, I know," Winthrop admitted, taking refuge behind his desk again. Looking somewhat proud of himself now that he was stepping back onto more familiar territory, he continued. "Mr. Dargient, his military adviser, also spoke with me at length. We had a long discussion about the hotel and their plans for it. Since the hotels are the main funnels of money into the Kormorelles, this island is off-limits. We have absolutely nothing to fear."

"Uh-huh," Barrabas said, leaning his hand on the back of his chair. "Seems to me you'd get along fine with Jim Bowie and George Armstrong Custer."

"Now look—"

"And if you keep thinking this way, you're going to see them sooner than you'd like."

Barrabas lifted the chair absentmindedly, then replaced it with a heavy thud as if he was using it to punctuate his words. "There are a lot of people six feet under who got that same kind of assurance from Captain Dargient. For now the island is safe, but when the people rise up and the tides turn against Dargient, that assurance isn't worth a damn. The hostages are here. They're the ace in the hole for Zahim and friends. Ransoms. Murder. Terror. Your guests provide quite a menu for terrorists."

"They're not like that," Winthrop protested.

Barrabas sighed. "Not here in the hotel," he said. "Not now. But on the other islands—" He spun the chair around, then sat down and leaned forward to look directly at the hotelier. "Let me tell you a bit about Dargient."

Barrabas proceeded to give him a different summary of Dargient's career. It was true that he was a hero in four or five countries, but it was also true that he was wanted in half a dozen more. Though his past employers disagreed about his morals, few of them disagreed about his skills.

After presenting a more rounded and accurate picture of the general's military adviser, Barrabas provided the final and meaningful conclusion. "He will do whatever he has to do to get what he wants. Break any promises, turn on any employer. Assurances, like those who believe in them, are the first to go."

The first cracks had appeared in the fragile armor of illusion that the hotelier had wrapped himself in.

Barrabas followed up by detailing the guests' vulnerability, which was Winthrop's main concern, explaining how easily they could be taken. What fate could befall them if no precautions were made.

He also talked about what would happen if Zahim went down and Daoud came back to power, but the most effective argument revolved around Winthrop's professional career.

Winthrop had spent his entire career to get to his current position. He'd turned several smaller operations into huge successes, pyramiding each victory into a higher position. He did it by genuinely caring for the customers, always going one step further than the other hoteliers in what he offered them.

That concern became the common ground for negotiating.

"The guests are your responsibility," Barrabas said. "If any of them dies, your good name will die with them."

William Winthrop sat back in his chair. He ran his hand through his wavy white hair, disheveling it in an attempt to regain his composure.

Barrabas didn't enjoy tearing down the facade of well-being that Winthrop had fabricated on the strength of Dargient's assurances, but it had to be done. At last Winthrop clasped his hands in front of him and leaned forward on his desk. "What do you want me to do?" he asked.

Barrabas studied him for a moment, then replied, "I want you to help me fight Zahim and Dargient."

"Perhaps I can stay neutral," Winthrop said with a faint hope in his voice. "Passing you any information that comes my way—"

"No," Barrabas said. "I need more from you."

"But I don't see how I can do anything. It's too risky."

Barrabas raised his eyebrow, staring hard, as if he could see through to the man he used to be. "You once were a fighting man, I understand," Barrabas said, bringing up what Mann had briefed him about the hotelier. "In Korea you were a much-decorated veteran."

"That was another time," Winthrop said.

"That time may have come again," Barrabas said, then added, "but don't worry. You don't have to actually fight anyone. You just have to let *us* get into a position to fight them."

"What exactly do you propose?"

"I suggest that you bring in a small team of trained security men—and women—to safeguard the hotel and your guests until the law is restored on the islands."

"Your men, I suppose?" Winthrop said.

"Not entirely," Barrabas said. "I have some key people to bring into the hotel. To make some changes, make this place ready when the time comes."

Winthrop nodded, coming face-to-face with the nightmare that had been lurking close ever since Zahim came to power. He was thinking of the work and the money that had been spent to create a paradise. And now it faced ruin. Though it wasn't solely his money that built it, it was his brainchild. He was the guiding force.

Perhaps, he admitted finally, the only thing that could save it was another force, a force represented by the man on the other side of his desk.

"Whatever you need," Winthrop said.

"Good," Barrabas said. "First I want to place some people on your staff."

Barrabas had selected a number of men still loyal to Daoud. He had also selected someone who could fit in with the guests but could still summon enough menace when it was called for.

"The man in command will be Claude Hayes."

"What will he be commanding?" Winthrop said, apparently having second thoughts. "An army of gunslingers carrying crystal carafes to the guests?"

"Relax," Barrabas said. "My people can handle themselves anywhere. They won't be awkward mercs in tuxedos." He smiled, trying to get Winthrop to loosen up. "They'll be graceful mercs in tuxedos."

After working out a few more details with Winthrop, Barrabas closed their meeting. As he was about to leave, Barrabas shook the man's hand one more time. "I'm glad you agreed to help voluntarily," he said.

Winthrop nodded, not particularly enthused. "And if I didn't volunteer?"

"Then I would have had to tell you that the Swiss company that owns most of this hotel is in turn owned by a man named Daoud."

Winthrop snapped his head up straight. "Why didn't you tell me that in the beginning? It would have saved a lot of time and trouble."

"Yes, it would," Barrabas agreed. "But I like to use reason to enlist people in my cause rather than the point of a gun. Of course," Barrabas added, patting the 9 mm Ruger holstered beneath his suit, "just in case, I always carry both."

THE SOBS were on reconnaissance patrol in familiar territory—a hotel bar.

The men were in camouflage garb, wearing well-tailored suits and the subdued shirts and ties of conservative businessmen. Leona Hatton wore a soft black dress that clung to her trim figure, with a deep slice of décollatage that invited a number of intrigued looks from some of the unattached tourists who were also patrolling The Island nightclubs.

The SOBs had taken up two tables. But they made sure the tables were separated by a fair distance so it wouldn't be apparent that they were together.

It was still early in the night, and in the corner of the bar a pianist was wending his way through the Modern Jazz Quartet canon.

Claude Hayes, a veteran of many Chicago and Detroit jazz clubs, was following the last notes of the *Fontessa* suite with a dreamy look on his face, almost as if he really were on a holiday like the other patrons of the bar.

But as a flood of soft applause swept from table to table, the real reason for the SOBs' presence brought him back to reality with a jolt. He shook his head, speaking softly in a deep voice. "Why me?" Hayes asked Barrabas. "Not that I'd ever refuse a direct order—"

"It's a direct order," Barrabas said.

"But I sure as hell don't see how I'm gonna pull off this majordomo stunt."

Barrabas shrugged. "I'm not worried," he said. "You're a classy guy, Claude."

"Yeah," Nanos said. "Or at least you can fake it for a while."

Hayes glared at the offender, but the stare didn't even make the brazen sailor flinch. Nanos, as was his custom after hurling barbs at one of the troops, had assumed an expression of total innocence.

Hayes knew he could handle the unusual role assigned to him if he had to.

Barrabas wanted him to join the staff of The Island Hotel and play the part of an official greeter, someone who got to know the important guests well and saw to their special needs. Someone who could shepherd them around, get to know them on a first-name basis.

On earlier SOB missions Claude Hayes had posed in a variety of roles, ranging from African ambassadors and statesmen to mercenary recruiters. He could play whatever role came his way but some of them, like the one that Barrabas had in mind, were too unlike his basic character for him to enjoy it.

Hayes lifted the tall stein of beer, then sipped slowly. He put down the glass and then smoothed his hands along the table. "Somehow, Colonel, glad-handing rich tourists who like to go surfing through the third world for kicks doesn't exactly make my heart sing."

"This isn't a matter of like," Barrabas said. "I need someone smooth enough to play the role, Claude. And then I need someone tough enough to bring down the curtain when the play's over."

Barrabas looked around at the wealthy patrons who were drifting into the bar, lured by the seductive music and ready to fall into a nightclub trance.

"A lot is going to happen here, Claude," Barrabas said. "There is no way the NKA will overlook this place. It's going to be a battleground, and I'll need someone to make sure we have enough islanders working here who know what to do when the time comes."

Hayes looked at the red-haired Irishman who was at the other side of the room. The former army captain and Billy Two were sitting on either side of Lee Hatton. Despite their suits, for all the world they looked like a couple of mild-mannered linebackers out on the town with the captain of the cheerleader squad. They seemed to be relaxed and as though they were genuinely enjoying themselves.

"I hear what you're saying, Colonel," Hayes said. "But O'Toole is tops in my book when it comes to training."

"Yes, he is," Barrabas said. "He's even a bit better than you when it comes to training. But you're still plenty good, Claude. Besides, there's something else I've got in mind here."

Hayes leaned forward. He wasn't worried about being overheard. The music and the general chatter of the patrons baffled the sound so that each table could only hear themselves talk. But even so, he was eager for any information that would add some spark to the role he had to play.

"The tourists aren't the only ones attracted to this place," Barrabas said. "From what our man Winthrop tells me, the mercenary leaders come here a lot. It's kind of a reward for those that Dargient can trust to stay out of trouble. Of course, there are a few who get drunk now and then and cause scenes, but overall there's a steady traffic of high-ranking NKA advisers."

"And?"

"And a lot of them hail from Kenya, Tanzania, all along the eastern coast of Africa. Dargient's haunting grounds."

"I get the picture, Colonel," Hayes said. Swahili was a language common to many of the eastern coast countries, and Hayes could speak the language like a native. He too had spent a lot of time on the continent.

In his role at the hotel, Hayes would be in a good position to pick up Intelligence from some of Dargient's free-spending, free-talking mercenaries.

"You want a little bit of Swahili surveillance."

Barrabas grinned. "Oh, I want more than that. Like I said, there's going to be action here, and a lot of it is going to revolve around you."

"All right," Hayes said. Though it wasn't his favorite assignment, he was definitely up to it. Besides, he knew that Barrabas never did anything without a reason. "I accept the position of majordomo."

"Congratulations are in order," Nanos said, raising his glass for a toast and Hayes and Barrabas followed suit. "Here's to Major Doom," Nanos said.

NIGHTFALL SHROUDED the glass-roofed restaurant.

The starlight was a magical special effect that added to the soft lighting of the room on the top floor of the Island Hotel.

For the past few nights, Claude Hayes had been welcoming a steady parade of big spenders into the exclusive dining room.

Hayes had quickly become a presence at The Island, his tall and lean figure clothed to advantage in the succession of suits supplied to him by the hotel's tailor.

The regulars vied for his attention, particularly the women who were intrigued by his aura of mystery. Though Hayes talked charmingly to one and all, he revealed little of his past or of his future.

To those who were more persistent about his history, he gave such a fantastic account that they would laugh it off. He was simply there, a man to welcome them, make them feel at ease. And though he never let on, he was still unimpressed by the cavalier spendthrifts who dashed through the restaurant and dropped small fortunes for a few hours of pampering.

Claude was particular about money. At times a wealthy man himself because of the lucrative SOB missions, Hayes always found a way to use his income wisely. He made it a catalyst for change. Whether it was contributing to a movement or founding one, he made sure that a good portion of his money did something for people.

That kind of approach hampered him a little bit when his job even called for him to encourage guests of The Island to throw away their money. It was like money dropped into a wishing well, and the only wishes granted were those of William Winthrop who had found a cash cow in the hotel that scraped the clouds.

After welcoming a number of now-familiar faces, Hayes retreated into the private suite at the back of the restaurant. Until recently it had served as an office, but Hayes had asked for it to be converted into a private dining room, small and cozy, outfitted with even more luxury than the regular dining room. It was the ''in'' place, an exclusive oasis in an already exclusive place.

Winthrop had protested at first, but when Hayes suggested that the renovation wasn't his personal whim but vital to his plans, Winthrop had come around, and the room had been refitted with lightning speed.

It had its own private hallway for access from the kitchen, as well as a fully equipped bath, which was already in existence when it served as a plush second office to William Winthrop.

A long curved bar full of glittering crystal lined the walkway toward a small winding staircase. The dining table was on a raised platform, giving it the sensation of being perched on a balcony overlooking the world. Through the long curved windows, the table had an unparalleled view of the Bay of Glass and the ocean beyond.

Hayes stood by the window, looking down at the water below and at the bright lights of the yachts bobbing at the hotel's private marina. Most of them were charters, but a few were ocean-worthy vessels belonging to the relatively rare breed of competent millionaire sailors, the kind who would crisscross an ocean on a whim, or sail down the Amazon.

They'd stopped here for a while, sidetracked by the latest paradise open for business. No doubt many of those yachtsmen would soon set a course for the private dining suite, Hayes thought.

Already it had attracted the attention of the diners, who gradually understood that someone who had the ear of Claude Hayes just might be able to gain entry into the reserved suite.

The exclusive enclave was in readiness, and Hayes had been informed by Winthrop that a special party would use the room and that Winthrop himself would appear with them briefly so Hayes would know the time had come to give them the special treatment.

They were due any moment, and Hayes was checking the room one last time to make sure it lived up to its billing.

After seeing that it passed muster, Hayes went back out into the restaurant proper—just as William Winthrop appeared with the special party.

Hayes wound his way through the lush pockets of plushly draped tables and glided over to Winthrop, who was standing with two women and a man in a white tux. The man was standing sideways so that Hayes couldn't see his face, although something about him was familiar.

The man turned just as Hayes approached to say "Good evening" and Hayes saw the grinning face of Alex Nanos.

Though Hayes thought he had Alex pegged as a seaman who was at home only in one of his fishing boats in the Florida keys, tonight he looked like a Greek shipping magnate who was fully at ease. Hanging to his arms like lovely tropical blooms were two beautiful young women.

"These are our special guests," Winthrop said.

Hayes harrumphed to himself silently, but he made them welcome and created a sufficiently discreet fuss so that many of the other guests noticed the new arrivals.

But some of the more enterprising women had already noticed Nanos, and a few of them sent subtly enticing looks his way. Though Hayes couldn't see what it was that attracted women to Nanos, there was something about him that never failed to do the trick. It wasn't the broad shoulders or the tanned and weathered face. It was the eyes—eyes that laughed at all comers, eyes that cast a loony enchantment over women.

Like the two that were on his arms right now.

Hayes recognized them as island girls from the village the SOBs had defended the other night. Most of the inhabitants had split up and moved to other locations on the islands. But some of them had ended up in safehouses, and some of them had ended up working at the hotel.

And two of them ended up in the company of Alex Nanos.

The women were dressed up in revealing gowns that were a world removed from the village they'd left. The beauty on his left wore a figure-hugging white dress that seemed to surge along her body, starting from the crest and swell of her copper-skinned cleavage. Her eyes were bright and sparkling, the eyes of someone who had been catapulted into another world and was eager to explore it. She moved easily, with a natural grace and the poise of someone used to being pampered, a princess in any world.

The woman on Alex's right was a bit more subdued, holding on to her emotions with a more veiled and slightly amused gaze.

Hayes was attracted to her. The first woman reminded him of a sacrificial lamb in the company of Nanos. But this woman reminded him of a priestess.

As he led them toward the private room, still maintaining his welcoming air, Hayes bestowed on Nanos a frown that no one else could see.

"What goes on?" Hayes asked. "I thought you were supposed to be on duty."

"Of course," Nanos said. "I am on duty. These are my bodyguards."

"Bodyguards?" Hayes said. "And who's going to guard their bodies from you?"

The women laughed.

Nanos tugged at his lapels. "Enough of this, my good man," he said, as they neared the back of the restaurant. "Show us your best table, this private room I've heard so much about."

Hayes escorted the trio to the back of the restaurant, then pulled on the gleaming handle of a sliding door. It made a soft sound as it slid into a recess in the wall, and for a moment the crystal-and-velvet interior was revealed to the room at large as Hayes ushered the guests into the private suite.

Those who caught a glimpse realized just how exclusive this special party must be.

It was working just as Hayes and Barrabas had envisioned. They had established the existence of a desirable private room, a room that would be in demand by the high and mighty. Particularly the officer corps of the NKA. They had also established Nanos's cover as one of the high rollers whose presence in the hotel would be expected. And for once Nanos had a cover he excelled at—that of a playboy.

Another SOB had made her presence known at the hotel. Lee Hatton had cultivated a devil-may-care attitude as she appeared poolside or at the bar. Perhaps an attitude that came to her easily. During her time between SOB operations, she was known to haunt the resorts of the rich.

Lee had been attracting attached and unattached men alike, men eager to impress her with their importance. Men like the upper echelons of Simon Dargient's private army, but Hatton had remained elusive.

Hayes closed the door to the private suite behind him and was about to say something to Nanos when the Greek cleared his throat loudly and looked around the suite with a skeptical eye.

"I suppose this will have to do," he said.

"Enjoy yourself," Hayes said, shaking his head at Nanos. And then he turned to the more subdued of the two women. "And you, lovely lady, guard yourself."

Looking deeply into his eyes, she spoke slowly in her lilting island voice. "Since you're so concerned, Mr. Hayes, perhaps I should place myself in your hands."

Hayes cocked his head sideways, smiling broadly at her. "I am here to see to your wishes," he said.

"Not on my time, genie," Nanos butted in.

Hayes bowed to the women, then backed out into the restaurant, where Winthrop was playing the part of benevolent patriarch watching over his staff.

It was all an act, Hayes thought, and a poor one at that. Many of the staffers were islanders—perhaps because it gave Winthrop a chance to crack the whip over the locals.

Hayes had sensed a prejudice in the hotelier right from the beginning. Probably the man's bigotry hadn't come out of any deep feeling, but simply out of tradition. He had been raised in a world where men like him commanded others. It wasn't strictly a color thing. Away from the public eye, Winthrop was overbearing with all the people who worked for him.

That inbred attitude caused some tense moments when Hayes began giving him orders. To be summarily ordered about was a slap in Winthrop's face.

But Hayes needed certain things done for the security of the hotel, and in that respect he brooked no disobedience. Hayes certainly didn't go out of his way to goad Winthrop. It just seemed to happen a lot when they were together because security was his province, and here, experience was the only king.

"I still think we should restore it the way it was," Winthrop had argued after the refitting of the private room had begun. "Let the NKA officers mingle with the rest of the guests. They'll feel at home and you'll pick up more information that way. It's a much more sensible concept."

Hayes had dismissed the suggestion with a shrug, but the hotelier never stopped complaining until the room was finished. Part of it was not wanting to give in to Hayes, and the rest of the resistance stemmed from his desire to hold on to the secondary office he'd been using as a retreat from the pressures of running The Island complex.

But Winthrop still didn't get the full picture why Barrabas and Hayes wanted the room set up. And neither of them felt like spelling it out.

Instead Hayes had explained a bit more of his philosophy of peaceful coexistence. "There are two kinds of people in the world," he said. "Live ones and dead ones. And up here, the dead ones are going to be the ones who don't listen to me. And they won't be dead by my hands, either."

That had been the end of the open warfare between Winthrop and Hayes, although there were still several clashes between the hotelier and his staff.

Winthrop treated the locals as children or thieves, as lazy natives who would never work unless he was on their back all the time. It was a skill he excelled at until Hayes derailed him.

On Hayes's first day in the hotel, Winthrop had been ranting and raving at one of the waiters in front of the rest of the staff before the dining room opened. The islander had stood there silently, not out of fear, but because he had to support his family. If that meant putting up with abuse, it was just something he was ready to bear.

Winthrop paced about the room with nervous energy as he yelled at the slighter and much younger islander. The tirade continued until he became aware of a large and disapproving presence.

Hayes had stepped up behind Winthrop, and was looking on with icy contempt.

The hotelier had turned around as if to launch another tirade, dismiss another person who had dared to displease him, then he saw Claude Hayes.

Winthrop stopped screaming, and Hayes said to the waiter, "Never mind him. He doesn't know better. Lack of proper education always shows."

The waiter stared at Winthrop who was sputtering out of control. Then the waiter turned around and headed back toward the kitchen.

"Yes," Winthrop shouted. "Go!" Then he turned to Hayes. "Don't ever berate me in front of my staff again."

Claude shrugged his shoulders. "Like you berated that man who's worked for you for years, in front of his friends? You're not only patronizing, but you're also abusive."

Winthrop shook his head from side to side, wondering what he'd done to deserve Hayes.

Undaunted, Hayes laid a strong hand on his shoulder. It was partially an offer of friendship or a warning demonstration of strength. He was prepared to either bury the hatchet or throw it. "You've been cursed is what it is,'' Hayes said. "Until this is over, I'm your conscience."

"I can do without that."

"You've been doing without it for too long, Winthrop," Hayes said. "So long that you can't even tell anymore."

The hotelier flushed. He'd been insulated from the real world for years. Who would ever disagree with him when one wrong word could banish him from paradise and back to another hotel haven?

Winthrop had spun about on his heels, then stormed out of the restaurant, slamming the door behind him.

Ever since that run-in, Winthrop and Hayes had observed a truce. In public they were friendly, and in private there was nothing said between them. It was business. They didn't have to like each other to work together.

As Hayes approached Winthrop, the veteran hotelier beamed a sincere-looking but false welcome.

"Keep smiling and I might just think you mean it, Winthrop."

The man's smile broadened. "I'm just doing my job."

"Me too," Hayes said, just as a pair of well-known NKA officers came into the restaurant. "Me too."

Hayes nodded and beamed a welcome at the officers who, like many of their peers in the New Kormorelles Army, had just come into a good deal of wealth.

As he headed toward them, Hayes managed to bury his real feelings. Rather than serve them, he wanted to sever them.

8

The ghost ship fled from Deadman's Bight while it was still dark out.

Though it appeared to have several passengers, most of the crewmen were actually nothing more than uniforms stuffed with straw or pillows, many of them wearing hats and propped up alongside the rails.

In the darkness and at a distance, the disguise would be perfect. But morning was only an hour away, and soon dawn would be chasing after the royal yacht, fully exposing it to daylight and to the bloodthirsty eyes of the New Kormorelles Army.

But it would also be exposed to the islanders who were formerly accustomed to seeing King Daoud's yacht cruising among the islands.

Part of the island tradition was waving to the king as he passed by on his pleasure boat—vicariously sharing in his regal life-style.

Since General Zahim had taken over however, there had only been a few rumored sightings of the yacht, but there were a dozen rumors about the fate of the king. According to one version, Daoud had fled the country for good and was living the life of luxury in

Paris. Another rumor claimed that he had drowned in the ocean after tumbling off the yacht during a drunken binge. One of the more gruesome speculations was that Daoud had been captured in the first moments of the coup, tortured, and buried in the grounds of the presidential palace. More secretive sources claimed that Daoud was alive and well, biding his time until he could make a triumphant return to take back the islands.

There was no end to the guesswork, but to most of the islanders, it was just that and nothing more. They couldn't live on rumors. They had to live on reality. They were getting on with life, adapting to the demands of the military dictatorship. They had to deal with the powers that be.

After all, where was their king? He very well might be dead. And if not, if he really deserved to be called a king, why was he in hiding?

True, there were some skirmishes on some of the islands, and there was a lot of talk about a royalist resistance faction, but as yet it was a secretive group, not open to anyone.

Some of the out islanders who seemed to be more knowledgeable about the resistance said that nobody heard about the resistance until it recruited him—or came for him.

Almost nobody knew that many of the rumors were spun in a tightly controlled propaganda mill run by the SOBs.

At the moment, one of the chief architects of those rumors was about to go public in a big way, and make quite a splash in the process.

Standing at the bridge helm, Alex Nanos piloted the royal yacht through the bright coral reefs that stretched just below the surface of the bay. The sea bottom was littered with other ships that had smashed their hulls on the relentless coral.

The waters of Deadman's Bight had scoured out a series of caverns, some of them submerged, some of them at sea level. The largest one offered a safe harbor to the royal yacht—once it had navigated its way into the grotto past the natural mine field of spiked reefs.

That was what had made it most attractive to Douglas Mann when he'd been looking for hiding places for just such an occasion. Like a rose with its thorns, the grotto was guarded by razor-sharp reefs.

Steady as it goes, Nanos thought to himself as he guided the ship through a claw of stone at the exit of the bight.

It was a treacherous pass for the multimillion dollar ship to move through. But Nanos wasn't worried. For one thing, it wasn't his ship. And at any rate, in just a short while it really wouldn't matter.

Heedless of the breakers splashing over the nearby reefs which protruded like a serpent's back, Nanos cruised through the claw, letting out a shout of glee as he looked behind at it.

Sea spray and wind swept the deck as the yacht picked up speed, knocking back a few of his ghostly crew. One of the straw-filled dummies sprawled out on the deck, his visored captain's hat skidding into the water.

Never one to believe in omens, Nanos barely gave it a thought as the dummy's yacht cap skimmed over the water. But nonetheless he made a quick sign of the cross on his broad chest and then, just to be on the safe side, threw in a prayer to Poseidon.

Up on the foredeck Liam O'Toole was peering into the weakening darkness, sitting calmly behind a swivel-mounted M60E1, holding the stock as calmly as if it were deep-sea fishing gear on a mount.

Nanos and O'Toole were the only SOBs on board. The rest of the SOBs assigned to the operation were already in position, along with Douglas Mann. They were all waiting for him at the end of the run. Or so Nanos hoped. Otherwise it was going to be a small invasion.

But Nanos did have some help from Daoud's private staff. On the starboard side of the yacht were two of the yacht's regular crewmen who had volunteered to come along.

They were both carrying silenced machine guns, the Mk5 Sterlings favored by Australian Special Forces. The weapons were part of the cargo the SOBs had brought with them from the Osprey, and Nanos and O'Toole had made sure both men had sufficient practice with the weapons before agreeing to take them on board.

Daoud's regular skipper had declined the chance to come aboard the yacht for this run, preferring the safety of the cave that temporarily housed him.

The Greek didn't blame him. Nor did he really want the man along. The skipper may have been fine when it came to escorting Daoud on his pleasure cruises, but sailing into a fleet of sharks was not his idea of a good time.

Under the circumstances the SOBs wouldn't have expected anything else. Only a fool would go on such a suicide mission, Nanos thought, as he increased speed and headed out for deep water.

Nanos kept close to the shoreline that he'd studied on maps for days now. He had also made preliminary runs in one of the IBS crafts, and he knew the waters, besides being aided by instinct. He was at home here, or almost at home.

Daoud's yacht was a bit plusher than he liked. The leather couches and the thick and soft carpeting throughout the salons were a bit much for his tastes, as were the cabins lined with silver ash.

But the well-stocked bars in nearly every cabin certainly seemed quite appropriate to Nanos.

Come to think of it, perhaps the king knew what he'd been doing all along.

It was a shame it would go to waste, Nanos thought. For soon the yacht would literally become a ghost ship. And unless he was careful, or if luck deserted him, he might end up as a ghost pilot.

SHOCKWAVES WENT THROUGH the islanders who saw the yacht cruising offshore early in the morning. The king had returned!

Sun glinted off the superstructure of the yacht, refracting from the array of antennae and satellite receiver poles and spreading out like wavering daggers across the water.

Word of mouth spread up and down the beaches. As the yacht cruised by the islands, villagers began streaming down to the shore, waving and shouting to their king.

The yacht continued full speed on its course, parallel to the coast of Mirror Island, creating a festival atmosphere along the hotel beaches.

The laid-back resorts weren't used to events like the return of a king. But many of the tourists who were awakened by the uproar, peered out from their balconies or joined the procession to the beach to personally witness the source of the outcry.

While many of the islanders were loudly sharing dreams of freedom once more, a good number of the tourists were thinking that perhaps now they would be invited to some of the legendary parties aboard Daoud's royal yacht.

The early-morning mist receded as the yacht raced past the Bay of Glass, heading straight for Grand Kormorelle.

And then it was shimmering like a vision as it glided along the shoreline of the capital city of Korvois. Past the open-air parks, the first modest houses on the outskirts of the city, and past the more elaborate residences that housed the hierarchy of the current ruling party, put into place by General Zahim himself.

Finally the yacht approached the main harbor for the Grand Kormorelles, which General Zahim had modestly renamed Port au Général. He had restricted access to the port to vessels used solely by the NKA.

The royal yacht looped outward to the left, then bore down straight ahead into the harbor where Zahim's armada of powerboats, utility boats and yachts was gathered.

By the time it was heading for the inverted U-shaped harbor, the streets in front of the presidential palace were awash with troops in sand-colored khakis.

A groggy General Zahim appeared on the steps of the presidential palace, with Simon Dargient beside him. Bare-chested, wearing only a pair of light cotton pants and sandals, Dargient was also riveted by the sight.

Like the general, he became charged with energy. But while Zahim was confused, almost panic-stricken, Dargient was delighted.

"It's the king!" Zahim shouted. "The king." He turned to Dargient. "What's he doing here?"

Dargient smiled. "He's committing suicide," he said. "How nice of him." Then he began giving orders to the troops milling about in front of him.

A detachment of mercs and NKA regulars ran from the palace across to the white church, then trotted down the steep cobblestoned hill that led to the harbor. They had to reinforce the idle crew below.

The few untrained and untested guards who'd been standing watch on the docks had done exactly that.

They'd watched in fascination as the yacht approached.

THREE SPEEDBOATS ROCKETED from their berths in Port au Général, whining past the bulkier and slower boats that were blundering about in the harbor. The narrow hulls of the high-performance crafts lifted out of the water as they raced toward the incoming yacht.

Each boat carried three or four NKA soldiers wielding automatic rifles that they fired wildly at the yacht. The target they had been looking for ever since General Zahim took over was now coming to them.

Liam O'Toole waited until the lead boat came into range before he opened up with the M60E1. Mounted on a tripod for sustained fire, the machine gun was belt-fed with a hundred rounds of 7.62 mm armor-piercing ammo.

The first burst chomped through the windscreen of the speedboat, dicing the glass and the upper torso of the man riding shotgun.

The gunner's arms were flung straight up as he toppled backward. The punch of the machine-gun rounds sent him airborne as the boat streaked for the yacht. His deadweight dropped into the water as his automatic rifle pinwheeled in the air.

O'Toole strafed the other boats that were roaring behind the first one, wanting to take them out or at least knock them off course before they slid under the field of fire.

Then he swung back to get the lead boat in his sight, pouring lead at the man behind the wheel. The wheelman was crouched low, but when the speedboat lurched and dipped after hitting a deep trough, the angle of fire was perfect.

O'Toole drilled him with a steady burst.

The dying man clutched the wheel, turning it sharply to the left. The speedboat careered out of control, almost turning over, but then settled into a circular course.

The Irishman whipped the machine gun back and forth, tearing through the hulls of the oncoming vessels.

The boat coming up on his right veered off slightly, then roared harmlessly out to sea, its blood-soaked cockpit carrying the shredded khaki remnants of the crew.

Liam O'Toole watched the last rounds of the ammo belt snake across the hull as he fired at the third speedboat. It had darted in a zigzag course and was now approaching the yacht. Three M16s fired at once as the craft drew alongside the yacht, aiming for the uniformed crewmen positioned along the railing.

Two of the yacht's dummy crewmen were decapitated, their ''heads'' tumbling back to the deck. A third crewman fell between the gap in the railing, his arm hanging down lifelessly until another burst from an M16 tore it off.

When most of the attackers' ammo was spent and the dummies were all shredded, the two islanders took their place on the side deck and fired controlled bursts from their silenced Mk5s.

It was a very successful effort, except for one thing. One of the wounded men shot back, sending his last shot through the forehead of the islander who'd just emptied his Sterling. The second islander swept the enemy craft one more time, putting down the NKA gunner for keeps.

The speedboat skipper pawed weakly at the steering wheel, spinning it to the right and accelerating away from the yacht when his end caught up with him in the form of hot lead.

CHAOS WAS IN FULL SWING at the harbor.

Unprepared troops screamed at one another as their boats ended up getting rammed in the attempted exodus out of the harbor. Only a few boats managed to slip out of the bottleneck.

Simon Dargient hurried along the wooden dock that paralleled the shore, keeping an eye on the Sudanese merc whom he had just dispatched to the pier on the right of the harbor.

The broad-shouldered merc ran toward the end of the pier, carrying an RPG-7V slung over his shoulder. Armed with a HEAT rocket capable of penetrating a foot of armor, the RPG could make up for the chaos suffered by General Zahim's makeshift army. They were used to raiding in boats, cruising along the coast, and the attack had found them unprepared.

The Sudanese merc angled himself for a clear shot when the royal yacht came in range. He knelt down and positioned the launcher over his shoulder. Then, almost as if it were part of a planned maneuver, he continued moving forward, pitching flat out into a prone position. His arms spread out like wings as the RPG slid across the dock.

His two Sudanese backups stared at the fallen man in wonder until they saw the bullet hole in his back and a dark rosette of blood spreading on his uniform.

"Pick it up!" Dargient shouted, and a second man reluctantly picked up the RPG. In a second he too was hit by a soundless bullet that caught him in the shoulder and spun him around. He tumbled off the dock.

Dargient scanned the farthermost pier, then looked beyond at the ridges and banks that made it a natural harbor. The rocky ledges on the right also made it a natural spot for a sniper.

Several more shots range out, whopping into the crew of a sportfishing boat just heading out into the bay.

"Corporal Gautier!" Dargient shouted, looking around for a man he could count on.

One of the sniper's bullets cracked into the waist-high stone wall behind him, ricocheting into the dirt at his feet. "Son of a bitch!" Dargient shouted, affronted that someone was shooting at him.

A split second later General Zahim screamed as a second shot cracked into the wall and sent a spray of rock splinters biting into his leg.

Dargient lunged toward the general to drag him to cover.

Zahim, who had contributed to the chaos by strutting around giving senseless and conflicting orders to his soldiers, looked panic-stricken now that the sniper's bullets began to fly.

Dargient sent him back to the palace with a few of his guards, telling the general his expertise was needed to direct the counterattack from there. Under the guise of going into action, Zahim retreated heroically in the direction of the presidential palace.

Nicholas Gautier shoved his way through a group of NKA soldiers that he'd been organizing, and hurried to Dargient's side. The corporal, a deceptively slender but powerful man, sported a brush cut, which only helped to reveal that someone once tried to part his hair with a machete.

Corporal Gautier flashed his veteran grin, and Dargient apprised him of the sniper concealed in the ledges on the right of the harbor. "Take Montfort and then take out the sniper."

"You want him alive?"

"Any way you can get him, Corporal," Dargient said.

Corporal Gautier turned around smartly and summoned Gerard Montfort from the crowd. Montfort was a much younger man, a man in his prime. He moved with the eager and heavy grace of an athlete who'd just made it into the professional leagues and wanted to prove himself.

"Slow down, Gerard," Gautier said. "You'll live longer that way. Or at least I will, and *that* is even more important."

Dargient's chief aides moved off in search of the sniper, while Dargient surveyed the harbor. Finally things were getting straightened out, and the fleet of ships was moving out toward the yacht.

His impromptu navy would take care of the yacht, and Corporal Gautier would silence the sniper. It would only be a matter of time now, Dargient thought. The king was making a grand gesture, a frontal attack on his former home. Grand but final.

Dargient looked out at the yacht. Then a shudder coursed through him when he registered the whup-whup-whup of an incoming chopper.

The Nightfox helicopter flew low over the town, hopping in and out of sight as it just cleared the spires and roofs of the houses.

A deadly metal rain fell, chomping up the cobblestoned road, shredding the wooden planks of the dock and scattering the NKA troops.

The chopper raced out to sea, unleashing a barrage of minirockets and 7.62 mm chain-gun fire.

The helpless ships exploded in geysers of flame all along the path of the Nightfox.

Then it circled back toward shore, dropping low to machinegun the troops, forcing Corporal Gautier and Montfort to seek shelter.

Dargient shook his head, raising the binoculars he'd snatched from a passing soldier, and scanned the waterline.

Out at sea he saw the royal yacht bearing down on the harbor... *while the crew members were diving overboard, abandoning ship.*

The yacht plowed onward, locked on course, crashing through the flaming ships littering the sea. A million-dollar torpedo, it was heading straight for Port au Général.

As the largely untried NKA troops were mowed down all around him by chopper and sniper fire, Dargient realized that the attack had all been choreographed. Every step had been mapped out ahead of time.

Whoever was behind the assault obviously had the know-how to have made it even more of a surprise attack if he'd wanted. A professional could have mined the pier during the night and blown it safely from a distance.

But the spectacle had been designed to make the biggest possible impact. An attack in broad daylight. The lazy approach of the yacht along the coast so all the inhabitants could see it . . . and then finally the flaming fiasco to show that the sleeping king still had sharp teeth.

There would be no king on the king's ship, Dargient realized, hypnotized as the yacht cruised closer and closer.

He came out of his fascinated summation of the event to shout "Fall back! Fall back!"

He shouted in French, English and Swahili, giving the order to everyone to retreat. His followers didn't wait to be told twice. They reacted quickly, eagerly.

The royal yacht went up like a volcano shortly after it smashed into the center of the pier, the blast of fire shrieking through wood and metal, blood and bone.

BARRABAS SQUEEZED OFF several more rounds from the Accuracy International PM sniper rifle. The Schmidt and Bender scope, along with Barrabas's familiarity with the 7.62 mm rifle, made life difficult and highly improbable for the two-man team stalking him.

But it was past time for his escape. The French mercenaries had come for him just as he was about to rendezvous with the midcabin cruiser that Billy Two and Lee Hatton had waiting in the water below.

Barrabas relied on that for his successful withdrawal, as did the men bobbing out in the sea.

But just as he'd been about to make the leap to the boat below, he'd scanned the area around him through the scope and seen the mercs approaching. They'd been running and crouching, tumbling and clawing their way over the ground, taking advantage of the natural cover as they headed his way.

They'd made good progress until Barabbas had pinned them down about sixty yards from his position. But soon the NKA regulars would join the mercs stalking him, and no matter how good he was, he couldn't hold them all off.

Scanning the ground in their direction once more, Barrabas slowly rose from the sheltering crevice.

He fired once, twice, backing away toward the edge of the ridge. He trained the sniper rifle on the last position where he'd spotted the enemy and squeezed off three more quick rounds until his back was to the open sea.

The mercs rose from cover just as Barrabas neared the edge.

He didn't have much choice. If he ran, his silhouette would make too easy a mark, highlighted against the sky.

Barrabas threw the sniper rifle in front of him, then dived blindly. He sailed off the edge, guided by his memory of the location of the cruiser.

As bullets flew overhead, he thumped down into the inflatable boat secured alongside the cruiser with a towing bridle and reinforcement lines. He landed with a rib-tearing impact that knocked the wind out of him. He'd made it.

Lee Hatton, clad in black camous, raised her Sterling SMG slightly and shot from the hip, firing a preemptive burst up at the overhang where Barrabas had just jumped from.

Billy Two stepped on the gas, speeding the cruiser out to deep water where the last of the royal yachtsmen were bobbing up and down in the water in their lightweight life jackets.

Douglas Mann made another pass overhead in the Nightfox helicopter, strafing the few NKA boats that were tentatively heading for the waterborne SOBs. The 7.62 mm slugs formed a dotted metal line through which the NKA fleet couldn't pass.

Nanos, O'Toole and their companion were bobbing up and down in the water, spread out with about thirty yards between them.

Nanos was the closest.

As the cruiser approached the swimmers, Lee Hatton dropped over the rail, landing in the IBS to be there if Barrabas needed help.

Barrabas felt like his ribs were on fire, but a bit of fire was nothing compared to pulling his men out of the drink.

As the IBS approached, Nanos kicked hard, lunging out of the water and bending his left arm.

Barrabas tossed the thick loop of the pickup sling over Nanos's arm. Nanos smacked his wrist with his right hand, hanging on for dear life as the sling towed him along. Using the momentum, he flipped himself up and over the side of the IBS.

The cruiser bore down on the islander, who'd been repeatedly drilled in the process by Nanos. He too raised himself out of the water, and when the sling looped around his arm, had a surprised look on his face as he clambered up and into the inflatable.

Nanos climbed up into the cruiser to make room in the IBS, and picked up a Sterling. Better ready than dead was his policy.

O'Toole's turn came last.

His ham-size fist thrust up into the air as the boat approached, and the sling shot him into the IBS as he repeated the maneuver.

Billy Two opened the cruiser all the way when the SOBs climbed aboard. His long black hair flew in the wet salty breeze as they headed out to the open, with Douglas Mann and his copilot flying overhead.

Behind them Port au Général was in flames.

The New Kormorelles Army had met the old SOBs.

9

Simon Dargient made the surprise inspection early in the morning when the Kormorelles were still swept by cool breezes and soft sunlight filtered through the mist.

As usual, Dargient gave no sign of displeasure as he passed through the barracks. Whatever was in his mind was locked away from the troops.

Dargient, Corporal Gautier and Gerard Montfort trooped up and down the lines, pausing now and then to bellow at someone with an unpresentable weapon, or lend a word of praise for someone who'd performed well in one of the recent skirmishes.

Ever since the attack on Port au Général, the islands had been the scene of raids and counterraids, punitive strikes on villages, and ambushes of NKA soldiers. Dargient had launched a campaign in earnest, sweeping through the Indian Ocean archipelago.

There really was a war on. It was waged against people who were fighting back and who knew how to hit and run.

Dargient was in the position of fighting against guerrillas who had assumed the role he usually played.

Now *he* was establishment. Now *he* had to lay down the law and keep order throughout the regime.

Every since the bullets started to fly their way, there was a drastic increase in NKA brutality and NKA desertions. That wasn't new to Dargient. He'd hired his share of mercs before who'd bolted for whatever reason.

Despite that, he had to maintain ongoing reliable routines and structures of discipline. Otherwise he'd always have a manic-depressive army. A good many of them already were past the psychiatric couch, with one foot always marching firmly on lunar patrol. There was nothing wrong with that. Some of the space cases made the best troops in action.

But he had to know what to expect from the troops en masse. Individually there were some standouts, and his own handpicked team were top-notch. The others, he thought as he left the last barracks, would need some more examples.

But first, before he could do that, he had to return to a large "power" breakfast back at the presidential palace on the main island. Once again, during the feast of fruit, wild pig and Arabian coffee, he would tell General Zahim how gloriously the war was going.

THE INFIRMARY for the mercenaries was situated on the far side of the compound, a converted barracks considerably removed from the active barracks. It was located close to the trees where shade could afford some protection during the most sweltering part of the day.

Fans also circulated air through the infirmary, plenty of liquids were available, and there was a well-stocked supply of medicine.

Dargient always arranged for a top-quality staff of medical personnel to attend to his troops. In the past, many an operation had failed because of wounded soldiers dying not from their wounds, but from lack of treatment.

And then there were the sicknesses, the epidemics that swept through troops thrown together, fighting in jungle conditions, trekking through swamps.

A good medical corps helped the mercs get on with their business. Of course, like in any business, there were always a fair share of bottlenecks.

Dargient quietly entered the infirmary shortly after noon, wearing a boonie hat and khakis just like any other soldier. The sweat and heat dropped off him as he stepped inside the room. It was a totally different climate, cooled by the fans indirectly stirring the air.

The infirmary was crowded with a few nurses and a large number of mercenaries who'd caught a bit of hell in some of the firefights. It was also home to a trio of cheerful mercenaries who had minor wounds that had sufficiently healed for them to be discharged. But they kept on coming down with a number of complications. Mysterious fevers. Long bouts of self-induced vomiting. They weren't sick around the clock. Just when it was time for them to be examined and evaluated for release.

Right now the trio of regulars were sprawled upon their beds at the far end of the infirmary. Their beds and a few others had been moved out of their neat rows, and the men were talking and laughing among themselves, playing it up for the rest of the mercs.

Dargient had nothing against the false bravado and wild humor that was often born of necessity from the bloodstained floors of the barracks. But the present scenario was different.

Dargient had watched these few ever since they'd signed on with him. They had thought they'd tumbled into an easy all-expenses-paid vacation.

They were always ready to charge into the bordellos, but when it came time to charge into the resistance, they always came down sick. And they always dropped into the infirmary to avoid combat, letting someone else do their dying for them.

Some of the nurses were obviously sympathetic and were eager to help them falsify the real state of their health. After all, most of the nurses were islanders. They didn't want foreign invaders to go out slaughtering their own people.

But on the previous day Dargient had the physician that personally looked after him and General Zahim come in for a second opinion. The doctor had checked out all the men in the sick bay, paying particular attention to the trio who had been making it a second home. The physician had had no doubt that they were playing possum.

Noticed only by a couple of nurses, Dargient turned to his right and slowly walked down the corridor toward the bed that blocked the pathway.

At the far end of the barracks were six men who had drawn their beds in a horseshoe shape, flanking a couple of ammo containers that were serving as a card table. One of them, a Dutchman whom Dargient had ransomed from a Kenyan prison, was laughing as he tossed a card onto the pile and raked in the pot toward him.

There were coins and bills stacked up before him. Scorch marks of cigarettes stubbed out on the thin wooden floor formed a half circle around his feet. Apparently he had been absorbed in the game for quite some time.

Dargient's presence was suddenly noticed. The laughter stopped, and there was a scraping of metal against wood as they inched their beds back into a semblance of order.

Dargient paused when he reached the group of card players. He looked down at the money, then at the black ace that had just been played on the top of the pile.

He faced the Dutchman, a brown-bearded rogue who'd been soldiering for ten years and obviously skating for most of them.

"Looks like you win," Dargient said.

The mercenaries looked at Dargient, then huddled back into their bunks, covering themselves with blankets and trying to assume weary looks.

The Dutchman was among the first to give in to the clutches of illness. Stretched flat out on the bed, a blanket up to his neck, he looked as if he were struggling with mortal pain while sweat dripped down his forehead.

Dargient picked up the patient record that was clipped to the foot of the bed. He scanned the Dutchman's record of alleged sickness, and the dose and schedule of his medication.

It was all unnecessary, according to the report of General Zahim's physician. It was clearly a con.

The Dutchman was a good actor for him to pull it off, or one of the nurses was in league with him, or perhaps it was a combination of both.

Simon Dargient rapped the clipboard, then spoke in his best bedside manner. "I see that, according to this, it's time for your shot."

Dargient tossed the clipboard down and reached for his Browning Hi-Power.

The Dutchman sat straight up in bed, flinging off the blanket, his gaze locked onto the sight of the 9 mm automatic.

Bam!

The blast knocked him back down on the bed, an explosion of red seeping from his chest to the white sheets.

Dargient fired a second shot.

Both of them had been long overdue.

Dargient looked around the infirmary. He thought of the men who'd died in combat. The ones who'd fought, just as these men were supposed to do, these men who had become extremely quiet and regarded him as though he were an avenging angel who had just stepped from heaven or hell into their corner of paradise.

Then, slowly, Dargient looked back at the freshly made corpse in the bed. "Now," he said to the Dutchman. "Now you need a doctor for real. Although it's much too late for them to help you."

He holstered the gun.

"I will not tolerate a *malade imaginaire* in this hospital," he said to the men. "If you have a real problem, yes, we will take care of that. We will make you fit again. That is the sole function of this installation. But no imaginary invalids are allowed."

He paraded down the double line of hospital beds, now and then leaning over and patting the shoulder of one of the genuinely wounded men. "If you really are sick, fine, stay. You will be attended to properly."

He wheeled around and headed back toward the trio of conspirators, one of whom was not capable of conspiring with anyone but phantoms.

"Otherwise, if you are not sick, then get up now and return to duty. There will be no punishment if you act now. However, if you are not sick and you stay, you too will be attended to."

Two of the beds were suddenly empty, as the Dutchman's pals scrambled for their gear, quickly rolling everything into a makeshift pack and heading out of the hospital. A moment later two more men gathered their things. They were slightly sick but still able to function.

Dargient nodded approvingly as they left. Then he looked at the white-garbed nurses who had drawn back and watched the movements of the mercenaries.

Dargient nodded to a stout nurse who had been particularly concerned about the welfare of the mercs who really hadn't been sick. She looked at him as if she longed to put him into one of the hospital beds.

Dargient held her gaze, amused by the fire she couldn't bring herself to scorch him with. In another country, another time, he may well have shot her for the insubordinate look. But he'd already made his point, and he didn't want the men to think he was totally crazy. Just crazy enough to keep them guessing.

"Nurse," he shouted, pointing back at the Dutchman. "Attend to this man. I believe he's suffering from an overdose of lead."

She hurried by him and stood by the Dutchman's side, eyes flickering from the corpse to the Dutchman's friends, then back up at Simon Dargient.

"Carry on," Dargient said, smiling serenely at her. Then he waved to the rest of the troops as he walked past them. As he sauntered out into the hot island sun, he sang a song from his legion days.

10

The secret brotherhood of the island nation had been cut adrift from one another, and as an influential group, from most of the Kormorellois as well, ever since the NKA had slaughtered their leadership.

They had removed themselves from the struggle against General Zahim.

The brethren, brotherhood, or returned ones, whatever name the islanders used for the warrior society, had become almost invisible, and the scattered pockets of the brotherhood hadn't done much of anything in concert.

Some of them retreated to the mammoth rain forests that towered over the islands, others maintained the guise of simple tribal villagers, fishermen and hunters.

Sometimes a few of them would ambush a stray NKA soldier, dragging the straggler into the forest and leaving his corpse for the carrion beasts.

But mostly they had been biding their time, as though waiting for a sign.

The sighting of the royal yacht was a meaningful event for them. Word of the assault on Port au

Général spread quickly through the main islands, and then hopped from island to island until the nearly one hundred smaller islands knew of the return of the king.

Speculation abounded. Was this the playboy prince? Or was it a warrior in hiding, a warrior emerged in the form of King Daoud?

The question had intrigued the brotherhood, who began meeting in secret once again. They established communication lines between the factions once more. Although it had been driven into hiding, the brotherhood was still intact. It was a secret society in need of a patriarch, a ruler to guide them.

For that reason, the brotherhood was receptive to the king's emissaries who had come to the outer islands in ones and twos, quietly hinting that there was a way to raise the brethren once more.

Gradually the brotherhood made it known to selected groups that they were willing to listen and possibly ready to fight.

There was evidence that the fires of resistance were spreading. The sudden rattle of gunfire bursting from some of the islands confirmed that conclusion. Skirmishes and drawn-out battles occurred with regularity.

Many of the brotherhood gathered on White Ridge Island. It was a significant location, a holy place baptized in blood. White Ridge Island was the spot where the first blood of the NKA mercs had been shed.

White Ridge was a perfect place to gather for other reasons. After the Tanzanian squad had been wiped out, the islanders had fled. The NKA swept through the deserted villages, torching most of them before searching futilely through the jungles.

Then the islanders had returned bit by bit, salvaging what they could from the destroyed villages and setting up camps in the tropical forests, where they could easily conceal themselves.

White Ridge Island was distant from most of the larger islands in the archipelago. A series of small atolls served as stepping-stones to White Ridge. They could also serve as lookout posts for any approach of the NKA—or the approach of the warriors who'd come to the aid of the king.

The brotherhood fully believed that Daoud was alive, and attributed the feat to the valor of his warriors.

What supported this new faith was the firsthand testimony of the islander who'd visited them. His name was Karloman Soleil, and he had actually been aboard the royal yacht and fired upon the NKA foreigners and turncoats.

Soleil informed them that the king was alive, that he needed them, and that soon there would come a man fit to lead the brotherhood.

Around a sheltered fire illuminating the pockmarked walls of one of the caves the brotherhood used for their councils, Karloman spoke of the fierce group of warriors who had been summoned to the Kormorelles by the king.

Their warlord was a battle-scarred man whose hair had been scorched white by the heat of the fight. He had soldiers who each had special skills he could call upon. But more important, the warlord had among his soldiers a special man. A warrior-mystic. Like the warriors of the brotherhood, he was allied with the spirits of the returned ones. He was guided by an entity called Hawk Spirit, and he had agreed to come to the brotherhood to see if they could come to an understanding.

The brotherhood was willing to see the warrior. If he passed their tests and that of their priestess, he could lead them. If he didn't pass, then they would mourn for him and give him a good burial.

SPEARS OF FLAME darted toward the Osage.

The shadows on the cave wall seemed to wrap themselves around his body, bathing him in darkness just as the flames from the small fire seared his eyes with light.

Salty beads of sweat streamed down Billy Two's face, oozing atop the animal oils that covered his body with a glistening sheen.

A leather thong held his hair back over his shoulders where it fanned out like coal-black tail feathers. Though he sat very still, cross-legged before the fire, the hawk was soaring within him once again.

The Osage was naked from the waist up. His upper torso was painted with bright splashes of red and green pigments in a stylized portrait of a hawk about to land on its prey. A large inverted triangle covered his chest and formed the body of the hawk. The wings splayed out along his arms. And the talons stretched down toward his center, the sharp claws flanking the ridges of stomach muscle.

Similar to the sweat-lodge trance he had often worked himself into back in his native land, the Osage was now in an otherworldly state—exploring the islands with his mind and with the eyes of Hawk Spirit, soaring above the battle sites, both in the past and into the future.

To Nanos, who was pulling guard duty while Billy Two communed with the local gods, the Osage was dabbling with delusions. Aside from that, the Greek was of the opinion that anything that worked with the warrior cult was fine with him.

The Osage had been meditating ever since the two of them had arrived on White Ridge Island in a small skiff during the night, following the directions to the cave that Karloman Soleil had given him.

It was a power spot, a sacred site, and Billy Two had picked up on that the moment he entered the cave. He'd sat through the night, sometimes chanting, sometimes just sitting immobile. Throughout the day the Osage had seldom moved from his spot in the interior of the cave. Now night was approaching once again, and he was still in a meditative pose, hunched over by the fire.

Alex Nanos was sitting in a slightly less meditative pose out by the mouth of the cave. While part of him watched the approach to the cave, another part of Nanos was meditating on the island girls he'd been squiring around at the hotel that served as their safehouse.

Most of the time the SOBs posed as tourists, and what Nanos missed most was living out his cover as a free-spending playboy, complete with a girl on each arm.

In his rumpled khakis, Nanos looked nothing like a playboy, nothing like a tourist. As he sat perched in a natural chairlike formation in a dripstone recess of the cave, Nanos held a Sterling submachine gun cradled in his arms in readiness.

A man with a demonic-looking face appeared out of the shadows. He moved quickly from the forest and stepped up to the cave. Despite himself, the Greek experienced a little thrill of dread at the sight of the man's face. It was painted red, like the river of blood that would soon be shed.

Nanos was silent. He was instinctively figuring out the best way to take him down if he had to.

A second face appeared on the right, painted blue like the mask of night. He, too, carried a double-bladed spear in one hand and wielded a long ceremonial knife in the other.

His eyes scanned Nanos and dismissed him quickly, then looked toward the interior of the cave. There was no fear in their eyes now that they had responded to the call of the warrior cult. They had reincarnated their fighting spirits which had been banished for far too long.

They moved to the left and right, not to flank Nanos, but to form a ritual gate for the priestess who now emerged from the darkness and stepped inside the cave.

She was an imposing figure. A string of bamboo sticks formed a necklace that plunged down between her breasts, which were caged but not covered by a snakeskin halter. Her jet black hair was crowned by a headdress of gold-lipped pearl shells, and her reed skirt split with every step she took revealing a stretch of firm flesh.

Her dark eyes glinted imperiously as she looked past Nanos toward the deep heart of the cave. She looked fully capable of wielding the pearl-handled knife sheathed on her hip.

"Hey, Billy," Nanos shouted as he got to his feet. "Your date's here!" Then he said to the three envoys of the warrior cult, "If you'll follow me..."

They split around him, the two men advancing first, the woman stepping slowly behind them.

"Or I'll follow you," Nanos corrected himself with a half grin. He moved in behind them, still holding the Sterling submachine gun. Not that he thought he would have any need for it now. The brotherhood had arrived as scheduled.

They advanced toward the interior of the cave.

The Osage rose from the cold floor, his huge silhouette momentarily blotting out the light from the fire, basking him in a halo effect.

Billy Two looked down at the two warriors as if he'd always been their chieftain, but when he looked at the priestess the trance returned to his eyes. She was an apparition from another world, and when she beckoned, he obeyed.

The quiet procession moved to the mouth of the cave. There they could see a long line of similarly prepared warriors emerging from the forest.

Billy Two knew that they would form the gauntlet when the time came. He had expected that. It was customary with certain cults—trials of strength and initiation. Before a man could lead them, or even join them, he had to live through their trial by combat.

As Billy Two followed the priestess, the two warriors motioned to Nanos with their spears. "You will stay here."

Nanos shook his head, then glared down at the armed might of the island brethren. "If he has to die," he said. "Then, I'll die with him." *And so will you*, he thought.

The two warriors understood that kind of sentiment and took it as a good sign that the Osage had won such loyalty.

Nanos joined their sacred procession, feeling somewhat like a heretic but secretly reveling in every second of it. It was like being on a movie set, and he knew that *someone* had to stay down to earth.

THE PRIESTESS'S NAME was Kamara, and after Billy Two had fought his way through the gauntlet—practically tooth and claw by the end—she led him back to the cave. Still standing guard outside the cave, all Nanos found out was that she was a dreamer, a trance dreamer for the warrior society.

The island brotherhood believed that the souls of their dead warriors were borne on the air, sometimes howling through caves, sometimes flying across the islands. Trance dreamers could communicate with those spirits. They could ask them for guidance.

Kamara had to get an answer about the Osage, whether he was a returned one, a warrior who'd come back in another guise. For her to receive their verdict, she had to be in close contact with him.

Nanos had lost track of the time and was almost groggy when Billy Two and the priestess stepped out from the cave. He'd been without sleep for too long, guarding the body and soul of William Starfoot II.

As they stepped out into the open, a line of brethren prepared the way with torches.

Aha, Nanos thought, seeing the Osage walk shoulder to shoulder with the priestess. There was a certain expression on both their faces...

The Osage looked clearheaded, and the mystic haze that had washed through his eyes these past two days was gone. And perhaps so was Hawk Spirit. *The bird has flown*, Nanos thought, but he kept it to himself. Now was not the time to reveal himself as a skeptic. Not when the warriors looked like they were finally ready to live up to their name.

Kamara raised her hand. She made the pronouncement that a returned one had come to them at last. A warlord was here to lead them. She told them that he'd come from far, from a continent an ocean apart.

Direct from the mental ward at Bellevue Hospital, Nanos thought. But like the other warriors he bowed his head. Mystic warlord or whatever, Nanos was ready to follow him. Aside from the friendship he felt for the enlightened Indian, it was part of his contract.

11

An invisible shudder affected certain people simultaneously when the two Kormorellois police officers entered the top-floor restaurant of The Island Hotel.

They weren't in their regular uniforms, though.
Rather they were in the uniform of the wealthy and the
elite, wearing cotton velvet dinner jackets and black
silk bow ties.

Until recently Commandant Limoux and his companion, a man known as The Bastard despite his deceptively pleasant name of Champagne, were both
minor functionaries in the police system of the Kormorelles.

Since the coup however, they had climbed rapidly,
by proving they were willing to do anything requested
by General Zahim.

Trained in the most effective interrogation tech-
niques by Simon Dargient, the two Kormorellois natives had acquired a reputation among their fellow
islanders that ranked right up there with the demons
of island lore.

But tonight they were smiling. Tonight they were
charming—at least on the surface.

The regular habitués of the restaurant were oblivious to the fear on the faces of the serving staff who were predominantly islanders. But the islanders knew all about Limoux and The Bastard, whose behavior suggested they were uncrowned kings who'd just entered their fiefdom.

Limoux was the head of the police apparatus, while Champagne was the head of the island Intelligence squads. For all practical purposes they were appendages of Simon Dargient's forces, but while it was true that he pulled their strings most of the time, they had done a considerable amount of damage on their own.

As a means of collecting bribes to fund their boundlessly growing desire for finer things in life such as clothes, boats, homes and fat bank accounts, the two men had charged anyone who crossed their path with being traitors and rebels against General Zahim. The accused could only prove their loyalty by offering substantial bribes in order to keep their wealth and their lives.

Limoux, a slender man who seemed incapable of commanding anyone without a gun in his hand, had longish graying hair that gave him a false touch of respectability.

Champagne was a different breed. Originally a back-street player, he was a fighter as well as a diplomat who understood the way the game was played. As long as you served the man in control, you could do no wrong. Your sins would be overlooked. With that in mind he'd always served the top dog while committing more than his fair share of sins.

The two men were raising a quiet ruckus with the staff member who had welcomed them to the restaurant. They were demanding the private dining suite.

"That's not possible," the man was saying as Claude Hayes drifted over to them.

He saw that both Limoux and Champagne were giving the waiter their most withering gaze, and there was a not-so-subtle air of threat about them.

Hayes glided in front of the waiter, then smiled down at the two intruders.

"That's not possible—*for most of our guests*—is what he was about to say," Hayes said. "But for you, of course, the suite is always available."

Limoux nodded.

Champagne shrugged.

"This way, gentlemen," Hayes said.

As they headed for the private suite, a blonde in a soft pastel dress that clung to her curves crossed their path. She was trying to be noticed, and she was. No question about it, Hayes thought as he saw both men give her a relatively restrained look. That is, restrained for a couple of sailors on leave, Hayes amended mentally.

He merely listened politely as one of them suggested that later on they invite her into the private suite.

The well-dressed SOB wasn't surprised by their manner. He'd known them from previous visits. On several occasions they'd been drawn into one of the hotel bars by Lee Hatton, who remained elusive—thus getting them to try harder and harder to impress their importance on her.

Hatton learned that Limoux and Champagne were in charge of genuine Intelligence and security matters, besides their sideline of extortion.

The cabinet ministers who'd been previously housed in the presidential palace had been removed to safehouses under their care. Guards were posted, supposedly to protect the ministers from rebels, but in reality to keep them locked in.

They had also jailed several genuine members of the island resistance, along with political prisoners. The tiny jail was so overcrowded that the surplus prisoners were either executed quickly or warehoused in residences commandeered throughout the capital city of Korvois.

They were thoroughly unscrupulous by anybody's standards, Hayes told himself again as he ushered them toward the private suite.

After he'd seated them, Hayes left them at the balcony table, assuring them that they would be well looked after.

When he returned five minutes later to see how his special guests were faring, he found them lolling about the table with an impatient and petulant air.

"No one's come in yet," Limoux snapped.

Hayes raised his hand gently. "I will take care of you personally," he said with an appeasing air.

With a good deal of show he selected a bottle of wine and opened it ceremoniously. He carried two long-stemmed crystal glasses to the table and then poured them three-quarters full.

"Where is the menu?" Limoux demanded.

For the first time Hayes allowed some of his displeasure to show. "In time," he said. "First I have a few questions to ask."

Champagne smacked his hand on the table. "Fool! Do you know who we are?"

"I know very well who you are," Hayes said to the thick-necked Intelligence man. "That is why I have some questions to ask. And for you to answer."

Both of them looked up with stunned expressions on their faces—no one had dared treat them like mortals in quite some time, and the lack of deferential treatment, especially from a waiter, left them shocked.

Hayes made a quick about-face, and the next moment he was covering them with a silenced M61 Skorpion machine pistol, which he was gently waving back and forth as if it were a divining rod.

Limoux was on his right, Champagne on his left.

They were darting glances at each other, trying to calculate the best way to attack. Hayes pretended to sail on, ignorant of their transparent attempt at communication.

"What do you hope to gain from this?" Champagne said, turning his chair to the right. His voice was a deep growl, and his eyes were coals of hate. Beneath the hate there was hope—hope that soon he would have Hayes nailed to the wall in his interrogation room.

"Speak softly," Hayes hissed, "or I promise it will be the last time you speak." He waved the barrel toward the Intelligence man, testing him. "Okay?"

"Yes," Champagne said softly.

"Much better," Hayes said. "I want to know the location of political prisoners of the regime, of the cabinet ministers and your own people you have imprisoned for fighting that eunuch named Zahim."

Champagne's lips curled in a half smile. "It won't help you any if we tell you everything," Champagne said. "So why don't you go back to what you do well—and bring us our menus?"

Hayes nodded in understanding, and his right hand darted to the left, coring the man's temple with the silencer and tilting his head at an awkward angle. "How about *sang du slug*?" Hayes suggested, digging deeper with the barrel before snapping it back.

The Intelligence man looked a bit more serious, particularly with the gouge mark from the silencer that was blossoming on the right side of his temple.

The man started to speak. And he spoke softly, with a touch of pleasure and pride, giving out names and places as though he were reciting a list of his favorite amusement park haunts. It was clear that he enjoyed dealing with people and their circumstances.

Hayes questioned Limoux next. The commandant also spoke freely, if a bit less exactly. Like his frame, his intellect was smaller than Champagne's.

When he was satisfied that they'd given up all they could, Hayes nodded and lowered the Skorpion. That's when Champagne made his move.

He lunged for Hayes's left arm, grasping both hands around his bicep, ready to pin that arm while Limoux attacked on the right to pin the other.

Hayes took a slight step back and to the right, drawing Champagne's grip forward so it lost power. Then he rammed his elbow into the man's forehead, and Champagne dropped down into his chair, his lights momentarily out.

Limoux was still in midair, lunging for the side-stepping SOB who now revealed that the Skorpion was not to be discounted yet.

The secret policeman tried to put on the brakes, but only managed to totter sideways, harmlessly passing by while Hayes drilled him with a 3-round burst to the brain. Limoux landed on the floor, blazing a trail of blood on the rug.

The phyyt-phyyt-phyyt sound brought the badly damaged Intelligence man back to life. He swiveled in his chair and clawed for his holstered automatic, but Hayes zipped him with a silenced burst from head to sternum.

The heavyset man nodded his head on his shredded breastbone, then tumbled forward, momentarily sopping the place setting with red before he tumbled out of his chair and sprawled on the floor.

William Winthrop, who'd been hovering about outside ever since the notorious pair had stepped into the restaurant, had been alerted by the vague sounds of the scuffle and came bursting through the door.

He saw the dead men, saw the blood all over the crisp tablecloth and the floor, and he saw Hayes standing there with the silenced Skorpion.

"What happened?" Winthrop shouted.

Hayes looked at the panicked hotelier. "The cheapskates didn't leave a tip," he said.

12

"Who are these people!" General Zahim demanded, shouting loudly enough to reach an audience of one hundred, though there was only one other man in the room.

Simon Dargient's expression was the same as if Zahim had spoken in a low whisper. The tantrums of tyrants didn't bother him in the least. But his mission did, a mission that was in danger of failing.

They were sitting in a fortress room in the underground tier of the presidential palace. General Zahim didn't feel safe aboveground anymore. Whenever he walked through the palace he always had the look on his face that he was expecting a nuke to come screaming out of the sky at any moment and demolish his headquarters.

The destruction of Port au Général had established a precedent of paranoia. When that was quickly followed by the disappearance of his top Intelligence chiefs, he was giving free rein to all of his fears.

Deep down, even Zahim knew he wasn't fit to rule. Without Dargient he would never had made it that far. Since he realized his military adviser was far more capable, he often wondered if the Frenchman was thinking of taking over.

Zahim had alienated the people of the Kormorelles, leaving himself without true allies and at the mercy of the warlord. Only the soldiers and mercenaries remained loyal because of the steady pay he was giving them.

But now with these losses, it was getting harder to keep the military in check. That was the problem with hiring so many mercenaries. Their loyalty only went as far as their own best interests.

"Who would dare do this to me?"

Dargient paced about impatiently, feeling restricted by the confines of the room. Unlike Zahim, he didn't like to be hemmed in.

There was practically an arsenal in the room, which didn't improve Dargient's mood. Zahim had a whole collection of pistols scattered about, some of them lying flat on tables like ornaments.

It was cool and damp down there. It was okay for snakes, for reptiles like Zahim. But Dargient preferred the hot sun overhead and the hustle and bustle of island life all around him. Rather than stay in hiding, Dargient's impulse was to go out and do something about the assaults. But Zahim didn't like to be left alone these days.

"Dargient! Are you listening to me?"

The Frenchman smiled, then raised his hand to his chin as if he were pondering the thought. "I guess I have to," Dargient answered, but he tempered the insolence with a more attentive look.

"Then give me some answers."

"Very well," Dargient said. He pulled out a wooden-backed chair from a table spread with a display of weapons. Then he leaned forward, facing down the beribboned general. "First, let me tell you who these people *aren't*," Dargient said.

Zahim was impatient, but he nodded just the same. He sat back and folded his hands together.

School's in session, Dargient thought, and proceeded with the lesson. "It's not the Russians, that much is for sure," he said. "First, they've got everything to gain by having us in power, thinking that we'll cut them in after the smoke settles and the blood is dry. And since Daoud has proven willing to work with the West, the Russians certainly wouldn't want him back."

Zahim nodded.

Both he and Dargient had repeatedly discussed how to deal with the Russians. They didn't want to rely on them at all during the early stages of the coup. Too much would be exacted in return. In fact, they didn't want to deal with the Russians at all, unless they absolutely had to. Dargient was not loved behind the Iron Curtain, and his personal experience had taught him not to trust them.

"And it's not the British. They washed their hands of these islands years ago. As for the French—" Dargient paused for a moment "—they are interested, but not obsessed with what happens on the Kormorelles. I believe they would like me here assisting you for no other reason than they know they can deal with me ... with us, that is."

"That leaves the Americans," Zahim said.

"Not officially, of course," Dargient said. "They would have to be free-lancers." From what little they'd seen of the men spearheading the resistance, they had all the earmarks of professional soldiers. But they were always in camouflage or combat gear.

"Someone like me," Dargient said.

"That thought has crossed my mind," Zahim said. "There were times I even suspected you," he added.

Dargient dismissed the thought. "I prefer to be a king without a crown," he said. "Fewer people try to kill you that way. The publicity if I were to assume power, under any name, would spark an outrage around the world. I would be taken care of quite quickly. No, General, I prefer to stay by your side. Together we'll be unstoppable."

In the early days of the coup the general would have agreed instantly. But now, with all the casualties around him, he was a bit slower with the enthusiasm. "Yes, Dargient, you and I ... unstoppable."

He spoke like an actor, rather than a ruler. A man reciting his lines instead of thinking them.

General Zahim returned to the subject of his Intelligence men. What if they had gone over to the other side? What if they had been murdered? Either way it wasn't a good sign for them.

"In time, General, we'll have those answers. First we must respond to the guerrilla attacks. This very afternoon, I am leading our troops to a zone where we have reason to believe the mercenaries are operating from.''

It wasn't a satisfactory response, and Dargient knew it. But there wasn't much he could do except attend to the guerrillas in the field. He had personally spoken with the hotel staff and several impartial witnesses. It was just as they said. A number of witnesses in the restaurant had seen the Intelligence men go into the private room and exit a short time later.

He knew that trouble was truly afoot. The inquiry into the disappearance of General Zahim's top Intelligence apparatus would have been much more severe if the NKA itself hadn't come under attack, and if the safehouses in Korvois hadn't been struck, leaving behind only a dead NKA guard. The entire group of cabinet ministers had fled. A great number of political prisoners had also been freed, spirited away.

All of his locations were hit in tandem, and the information had to come from Limoux and Champagne.

Dargient shook his head. It was not a good situation. The other side had just gained a number of dedicated reinforcements.

After all the ill-treatment they'd received at the hands of the NKA, they would be willing to fight to the death—a death they'd so recently avoided because of their rescue.

But General Zahim was still in power, and that was the important thing, Dargient thought. Soldiers died, which was the natural course of things. And rulers ruled, whether they were seated upon the throne or operating behind it.

"Rest assured, *mon général*," Dargient said as he pushed away from the table. "We will take care of these . . . these rabble-rousers."

His initial amusement at having someone sufficiently skilled to offer him a challenge had quickly evaporated. But he hid that discomfort from the general.

"You see," Dargient said. "The mercenaries, whether they are Americans, or other free-lancers, are obviously working with the cooperation of our friends on Mirror Island. The hoteliers and the bankers, they are the backers, no doubt. But that will be taken care of in time. After we return from battle, we will march on the last outpost—the hotels themselves."

Zahim looked surprised. Earlier Dargient had insistently cautioned him about moving against the tourists. That was where the main source of income to the islands came from.

"Some of the tourists will surely get hurt," Dargient said. "That is unavoidable. But we can always blame that on the rebels. The terrorists. Once order is restored, we can open the doors to paradise once more."

But before the doors to paradise could reopen, he thought, there would have to be a blood payment.

THE FIRES WENT OUT at White Ridge Island with the coming of night. Like many of the other clandestine settlements, the villages of the warrior society were not real villages anymore. Rather, they were a cluster of lairs dug out of the earth.

Grass-covered corbeled roofs camouflaged the homes that were built into the sides of hills, or the huts and trenches and lean-tos that were built into the jungle.

Then there were the caves. Some of them had long galleries that led underground. Others had streams that merged with the sea.

The maze of tunnels had become a second home to the warriors who were long used to conducting their affairs in secret, and now they could use them as a base to conduct their wars in a likewise manner.

In many places the rain forest had been undisturbed for so long that the trees that had died and toppled never fell very far. They were intertwined and supported by the living foliage, forming a canopy of concealment above and a labyrinth below which few could follow.

But the islanders who'd spent most of their lives nearby the great forests knew their way through, and whenever the NKA approached, they could vanish in a matter of minutes. And if the NKA approached too far and stepped into the jungle, they often failed to return.

It was the home of the brotherhood.

The island was also the new home of many of the freed Kormorellois. The overflow of ministers and political prisoners who couldn't be concealed in the safehouses were moved through an underground network that stretched from White Ridge to the outer islands.

For many of them, truly living in the bosom of nature was a culture shock, but for others it was a rebirth.

There was plenty to live on. Tubers, wild yams, bamboo shoots, fruits. And there was wild game for those who were swift enough to trap them.

All in all, it was a temporary return to paradise, making the Kormorellois refugees understand just what they stood to lose if the NKA prevailed.

It was a rough life for some of those who had grown soft in the city, but no one was going to complain about the accommodations, especially since a lot of reports indicated that the NKA were beginning a crackdown on Grand Kormorelle.

They were also sweeping through the main islands to scout out the resistance. On the outer islands they were especially brutal. The farther they got away from Grand Kormorelle, the more ruthless their methods. There was no one to see what happened, no tourists to worry about.

But it was also on the outer islands that the sleeping dragon had awoken. Billy Two and the warriors of the brotherhood had made their presence known in a series of skirmishes with the NKA.

Resistance was coiling through the Kormorelles like a noose, and sooner or later Zahim's army would find itself in a showdown with the alliance of the SOBs, the brotherhood and the Grand Kormorelle refugees.

The morale of the resistance was high, boosted by the long overdue demise of Commandant Limoux and his sadistic associate, Champagne. There was justice, after all, was the general consensus.

Together the two hatchet men had created too many ghosts among the Kormorellois. It was most fitting that they had met their end in The Island's private dining room that they had demanded admittance to.

The story had quickly spread among the resistance and was retold frequently to boost morale...

As the hotelier William Winthrop had stood around in a daze, two natives stepped into the private dining suite through the staffer's entrance. As previously arranged by Claude Hayes, the islanders were in their finest evening wear, just like the clothes that the general's hatchet men had worn.

A short while later, two very noticeable women acted tipsy and loud as they made a big entrance in the top-floor restaurant. Claude Hayes escorted them to the private suite, as though the women were summoned by the hatchet men.

About a half hour later an apparently drunken party of four emerged from the dining suite, quickly heading past the other guests. They were shadowed by Hayes and Winthrop so no one could get a good look at them.

The foursome took the elevator downstairs, and the hatchet men were seen no more.

The corpses of Limoux and Champagne made their exit in a more discreet fashion, bundled into a service elevator and then sneaked aboard their yacht. The yacht then cruised out of the marina and vanished.

There were some reports of a loud explosion at sea, but there were no remnants.

The fate of the Intelligence chiefs remained unknown to the general, stoking up his paranoia. Especially when the subsequent raid freed the ministers. It seemed as if the Intelligence men were alive and working for the other side, an illusion the SOBs were eager to maintain.

Psychological warfare was just as vital as the real warfare that the SOBs waged so well.

13

The invasion of White Ridge Island began early in the morning, when a half dozen Kormorellois fishermen spotted General Zahim's makeshift fleet in the distance.

The word quickly spread to the rest of the people gathered on White Ridge. Included in their number was the toppled king. Until then the place had been a safe harbor for Daoud.

An armada of powerboats, cruisers, fishing boats and well-preserved two-masted brigantines approached from the south end of the island. The brigantines had formerly been a means of transport between islands, but in their new capacity they were transporting NKA soldiers.

Nile Barrabas gazed through a pair of waterproof Fujinon binoculars at the advancing navy.

The lead boat was a fly-bridge motor yacht that carried several crewmen in sand-colored khakis, and a man Barrabas took to be Simon Dargient, but Barrabas only had a fleeting glance before another boat blocked his view.

He scanned the other boats that covered the horizon, which was a mass of masts and sails and steel-spined conning towers. Some appeared to be carrying supplies as well as troops.

It certainly was unlike the other scouting raids that had come to White Ridge Island. They were prepared to stay for a while.

Standing at the edge of a sliver of jungle that wound down to the sea, Barrabas flipped the lens caps back in place on the lightweight marine binoculars and let them hang from their straps.

"Get Billy Two," Barrabas said to Alex Nanos, who stepped back through the trees to summon the Osage.

Since Billy Two had established the most rapport with the Kormorellois natives, Barrabas had assigned him the task of leading them into skirmishes.

The Osage appeared a few moments later, accompanied by three of the brethren. They carried long bows that were taller than they were. The spear-length arrows seemed unwieldy, but Barrabas had seen them in action on the Kormorelles, as well as in the African bush. They could split a man in two. There were few minor wounds made from such an attack.

Billy Two was armed with his laser-sighted crossbow, a bit of magic that had hypnotized the warrior cult when they'd seen it in operation.

"I want a limited response here," Barrabas said. "If it does come to that. I'm going to try and divert them for now, but if they land in force, meet them with a skirmishing party, then fall back into the jungle. Unless they penetrate the caves where the women and children are, I don't want a battle royal here. Don't give away our full strength.''

The Osage nodded. He'd forged a small unit into a top-flight guerrilla band. They could engage the enemy and lead them into the interior, hopefully ending up with a lost army of NKA soldiers, who thought they had discovered a raiding party, rather than the main refuge of the loyalists.

''We're not ready for a showdown yet,'' Barrabas said. ''If they pinpoint us now, they can hold us down until reinforcements arrive.''

The Osage looked out at the task force riding the crests of the waves. A few of the scouting boats were already far ahead and would reach the island in a matter of minutes.

''What's your diversion?'' Billy Two said.

''We'll take the CAT,'' Barrabas said.

Like the Nightfox, concealed in a makeshift hangar of bamboo and vines deep in the forest to prevent it from being seen by flights over White Ridge, the CAT 900 assault craft was also hidden. The SOBs had created a hidden mooring for it beneath an outcropping of jungle.

The CAT was a high-speed assault vehicle but the look in Billy Two's eyes said that the odds were too great. ''You going to surround them?'' he asked.

Barrabas laughed. ''No, but we're sure as hell gonna spook them. Let them think they flushed a small patrol. Maybe they'll come after us.''

''Good luck, Colonel,'' the Osage said.

Barrabas cocked his head and remarked with deliberation, "The hell with luck." Ever since Billy Two had been accepted by the brethren, the island warriors had been treating him like a demigod. "Couldn't you spare a thunder bolt or two?"

Billy Two laughed. "I'll see what I can do," he said. Then he clapped Barrabas on the shoulder. "See you in a while," he said. But the look in his eyes warned that the next time they met each other might be in another world.

THE CAT 900 ROARED out of the bay like a gleaming white torpedo. The thirty-foot catamaran's narrow hull, designed for aerodynamic lift, was angled toward the sky as it smashed through the waves.

Nanos opened it up, screaming toward the armada. Just as the catamaran came into firing range, the Greek seaman swung to the right.

The SOBs unleashed a barrage of automatic fire onto the NKA fleet, but at that point it was more to sting them than to do any real damage.

O'Toole and Lee Hatton cut loose with several bursts from their M-16s, while Barrabas emptied a 10-round magazine of 7.62 mm Nato slugs from an Accuracy International Model PM. The L96A1 sniper rifle dropped two NKA crewmen from the fly-bridge yacht who'd been startled enough to stare in shock at the high-speed CAT.

"All right, Alex," Barrabas shouted. "Do your stuff."

"My pleasure, Colonel," Nanos said, giving it full throttle.

The CAT 900 sped away at nearly sixty knots in a pretense of flight from the armada. Several ships broke off from the fleet in pursuit.

Liam O'Toole sat across from Barrabas, holding the barrel of the M-16 skyward.

"It's working, Colonel," the red-haired Irishman said, looking at Barrabas for confirmation.

Lee Hatton had the same question on her mind. "Yeah," she said, shouting over the drone of the engine. "If you wanted to get them all interested in killing us, you've got your wish."

Barrabas nodded. "We'll lead them to Maku Island. Go inland, stage some fireworks, and then hopefully leave them there."

It was one of the fallback plans the SOBs had set up ever since they'd organized the Kormorellois.

Like many of the nearby islands, Maku had a cache of arms. It also had a squad of resistance fighters ready to use them. Once the SOBs hit the island, they would activate the Kormorellois squad and try to raise enough hell to make the NKA think it was their main staging area.

In theory the plan was simple. The SOBs could radio the Nightfox to back them up if they needed it, although from the looks of it, Douglas Mann might have to pilot the chopper against the White Ridge landing parties.

A crashing wave flooded over the CAT 900, drenching the SOBs as Nanos sliced it across a rough stretch of deep troughs.

"There's the reef," Nanos yelled above the noise. "Dead ahead."

"Nice choice of words, Alex," Hatton said as she stepped to the back of the boat with Barrabas and O'Toole.

The CAT 900 roared toward a gap in the coral reef ahead, wide enough for two boats to shoot through. A misjudgment at high speed would result in gouging the hull and leaving them stranded.

Nanos slowed down as they approached the gap— not because he wasn't sure of streaming through there safely—but because they wanted the pursuers to catch up to them.

The SOBs carefully lifted a line of buoys that Nanos and Hayes had prepared for just such an occasion. As a veteran UDT man, Hayes had rigged up a fishing line of mines to go "trolling for terrorists," as he called it.

Attaching them to a half dozen plastic floats similar to the kind used to track underwater divers during training missions, Hayes had transformed a handful of Bangalore torpedoes into impact mines. The thin steel tubes of explosives descended from lines attached to the floats. Painted sea green, the floats acted like buoys.

Nanos zigzagged so the pursuers couldn't quite see what his crew was up to. At that moment the SOBs tossed the buoys overboard.

The CAT 900 passed through the gap in the reef, lingering just long enough to stoke the blood lust of the closest pursuer.

The lead NKA vessel was a deep V-hull sportfisherman with two men behind the wheel and a trio of gunners in the cockpit. They'd reached the spot in the reef a few moments after the SOBs closed the door.

The yacht snagged the lines, levering the Bangalores upward like pendulums where they hammered into the hull and detonated.

Like hand grenades blowing fish out of a pond, the TNT and amatol mines blew the NKA soldiers into the air, shredding them with metal and fiberglass shards.

While the rest of the crew was disintegrating, one of the soldiers flipped down into the water—just in time for a sleek black speedboat to thump into him. It sailed through the shower of metal and fire before it gored itself on the reef.

A second huge blast punctuated the momentary silence, almost vaporizing the speedboat and sending a pink-tinged spray into the air.

As the CAT 900 roared off toward Maku Island, the hunters gathered by the reef, no longer hell-bent on catching their quarry at sea. Instead they took the slower route, cruising out around the reefs. It would take them longer to get to Maku Island, but they could still keep the CAT 900 in sight.

Barrabas swiveled in his seat, scanning the horizon with the binoculars.

Dargient had taken the bait—perhaps too well. The NKA fleet stretched out on the horizon, silver and white hulls gleaming in the sunlight as they bobbed up and down.

Rather than send out just a diversionary force in pursuit of the CAT, Dargient was sending most of his ships after it, figuring that the men in the CAT were the ringleaders.

Dargient knew the resistance would collapse if he crushed the leadership.

Cut off the head and the body dies—not a bad philosophy, Barrabas thought. But he didn't want to give the Frenchman a chance to prove it.

KARLOMAN SOLEIL jumped out from the thick brush along the riverbank as the CAT 900 floated downstream. With him were a half dozen other Kormorellois loyalists. Grabbing the mooring lines, they hauled the catamaran into a small sliver of water that splintered from the stream and quickly covered it with foliage.

They helped Barrabas and the SOBs distribute the packs, weaponry, and radio gear that had been stowed away in the catamaran.

"I got everyone ready when we heard the explosions," Karloman said. "We figured the NKA would come here next."

"You figured right," Barrabas remarked approvingly. "And they're coming in strong."

Karloman nodded, rubbing the back of his hand against the stubble on his chin. His somewhat boyish look was overwhelmed by all the weaponry he carried.

He was draped with spare magazines and flares taped to his belt, a knife, side arm and the Sterling SMG he'd proved so proficient with during the assault on Port au Général.

"Glad to see you're dressed for the occasion," Barrabas said, glancing down at the weaponry. "Unfortunately it looks like you're gonna need every bit of it."

"We're ready," Karloman said.

The men with him were similarly armed and had a number of grenades that Barrabas had previously distributed among them. Karloman and the other loyalist soldiers wore tiger-stripe camous that blended in with the strips of jungle covering Maku.

The party of SOBs and loyalists moved quickly into the jungle, joined along the way by several other Kormorellois who'd been based on the island.

It didn't take long to reach a sun-baked plateau where they could look down upon a good stretch of shoreline.

Maku was an inhospitable island with a maze of thick jungles, several enormous cliffs and slabs of volcanic rock piled up like enormous steps meant at one time for giants who no longer walked on the island. Several active streams cut through Maku, along with a half dozen almost dry riverbeds.

There was one strip of white sand along the western coast of the island that looked inviting, especially to the fleet of NKA ships that were dropping anchor.

Barrabas scanned the horizon as scores of figures leaped out of the boats and ran ashore.

With deft movements he wrapped a bandana around his coarse white hair, slapped a fresh magazine into a Sterling SMG he'd brought from the boat and then slung it over his shoulder. He still carried the Model PM sniper rifle, painted in splotches of sand brown and jungle green. He also had a wide assortment of grenades and Claymores.

Each of the SOBs was a walking armament factory—a factory about to strike.

O'Toole stood beside him, observing some of the NKA figures scrambling over the beach and peering behind each rock and crevice as if they were playing hide-and-seek.

He also watched a group of Sudanese mercenaries very matter-of-factly stalking into the jungle. Appearing behind them was a man who seemed to be giving orders. He was always moving, positioning the NKA and the mercs along the beach.

Some of the yachts sailed parallel to the coast, dropping off patrols to scout through their sectors.

Karloman Soleil clambered up beside Barrabas to take a look. Apparently he didn't care for what he saw. The sight of the soldiers caused him to grunt out loud like a man with a fear of heights who'd suddenly found himself stranded on a windswept bridge. "We're dead," he said.

"Keep thinking like that and you'll be more of a prophet than you want to be," Barrabas remarked reprovingly.

"But look at them all!"

"I've seen them," Barrabas said. "I've seen them here, and I've seen them in a dozen other places just like that. And I'm still here looking at 'em. You *can* live through this, Karloman."

"How?"

Barrabas studied the young man. He'd been in several skirmishes already and had proved himself. But this was the first time he'd faced such overwhelming odds.

"Do unto them before they do unto you," he said. "Come on."

The SOBs worked their way through the jungle. Setting up Claymores. Digging in sniper positions. Throwing obstacles along the main pathways. They didn't have the numbers but they had knowledge on their side. They'd scouted the island and knew the lay of the land. They knew the direction from which the NKA would most likely come, and the routes of retreat after an ambush.

No matter where they would head, death was waiting for them at every step.

NILE BARRABAS HURTLED through the clearing, running in plain sight of the NKA patrol.

It was just a brief exposure, long enough for him to be spotted and for the enemy to think that they had their quarry on the run.

Barrabas fired off a burst from the Sterling as his feet thundered over the high grass and kicked into the tangled vines at the welcome rush of jungle wall.

Several shots ripped through the clearing, chomping into the undergrowth. When there was no return fire, the NKA soldiers leaped forward. Seven of them charged over that same clearing, moving into the jungle, calling for others to join them.

It was like playing a lottery to see who would get the prize first. But then their number came up.

As Barrabas knifed through the last thicket of brush and dived for cover, Liam O'Toole hammered his palm down on the clacker that was connected by fifty feet of wire to the Claymore mine planted along the path Barrabas had just taken.

The mine went off, sending a steel stream of pellets into the onrushing NKA patrol, shredding flesh and bone and knocking the soldiers off the path.

Barrabas and O'Toole came back through the forest unseen, firing Sterling submachine-gun bursts at the patrol to finish off anyone who'd survived the Claymore blast.

M-16's chattered all at once, sending a stream of automatic fire through the woods.

The NKA rangers laid down a deadly barrage into the jungle that would have killed anything in their path.

But there was *nothing* in their path. Nothing but ghosts and their own paranoid projections as they fired into the jungle, wasting their ammunition and racking up a body count of phantoms.

After they spent most of their ammo, they heard real fire in the distance as NKA soldiers screamed and fell, and the loyalist jungle fighters moved closer.

A CALM DESCENDED on the island. There had been no fire for some time now. Taking advantage of the lull, a thirty-man force of NKA troops sliced through the jungle, spread out in a long single file.

Some of them moved cautiously while others moved with abandon. The inexperienced soldiers who'd been dragooned into the NKA forces stepped a bit more confidently, thinking that finally their quarry had seen the light and were slipping away from them.

The veteran mercs who accompanied them however, knew that it was just the calm before the firestorm.

A moment later they knew they had been right when they heard the first few drops of deadly metal rain.

It started like a pitter-patter. One shot. Two shots. A 3-round burst.

And the NKA troops began to fall.

Planted behind a low ridge, their bodies covered with shrubbery and their faces streaked with mud and camouflage paint, Lee Hatton and Alex Nanos were busy chopping up the patrol.

They'd taken out the most dangerous ones first, Nanos picking off a stocky mercenary who'd been walking on the flank carrying a heavy machine gun. At the same time, Lee Hatton had her sights on the NKA radio operator, knocking him off the air and into the next life with a shot to the forehead.

Each of them was armed with a Colt Commando, using the short-barreled assault rifles with such accuracy in close that they dropped nearly a third of the patrol before they moved back into the jungle.

As the patrol picked itself up and turned to their left to begin stalking their ambushers, Liam O'Toole appeared to their right. The Irish army captain wielded a Daewoo USAS-12 automatic shotgun that punched holes in trees and chomped through everything in its way as though it was paper. He stood his ground, dropping the three NKA soldiers closest to him, then taking out two more who dived into the brush, firing ill-aimed bursts at him.

Then O'Toole moved through the jungle, letting the entire 28-round drum rip through the shattered patrol.

Finally he stepped back into the woods.

It was a game of hide-and-seek—the full-auto lead seeking out the NKA with hideous accuracy.

The SOBs knew the game well. Hit and run. Raise hell and send them to hell. Then vanish.

It worked well, but by necessity they were being split up as more and more of the NKA troops landed on the island.

And the battle wasn't entirely one-sided.

Karloman Soleil had been waiting in an ambush they'd set, watching the progress of a single-file line of NKA soldiers approaching. But the soldiers moved slow. Too slow. As they plodded forward, a swift team of Sudanese mercs had circled behind the loyalists.

They'd opened up at almost point-blank range, gunning down Soleil's comrades in the back. They fell all around Soleil, their dying bodies tangled in vines, their blood-inflamed eyes vainly searching for the assassins who'd put them down.

Soleil turned into a madman, firing 3-round bursts of the Sterling in a steady arc in front of him. He moved forward, hitting two of the Sudanese mercs off to his left side. Then he diced another one who'd just finished a comrade.

As the NKA soldiers who'd been walking in single file neared, they dropped down and began firing in Soleil's direction.

Soleil scrambled through the brush, moving toward the enemy line with Barrabas's golden rule in mind, of doing unto them with full-auto. He made it through the NKA encircling movement, knowing that at best only a handful of other loyalists had survived.

It seemed like the entire island was engaged.

He knew what the intention was—to draw as many of the NKA here as possible. But it looked like success meant death.

Still, whenever he heard the other bursts slicing through the jungle, he knew the SOBs were still alive and dealing death.

He headed toward the last skirmish, knowing that he would find either friend or foe there, knowing that it was likely he would be killed. But if Karloman Soleil didn't fight now, he also knew that he would probably be killed in a much more brutal way in an NKA holding cell.

AFTER TWO HOURS of fighting, Barrabas and O'Toole linked up with Hatton and Nanos.

The NKA had suffered incredible casualties, but their sheer numbers had insured that many of the Kormorellois would fall.

When there were just a few of them left, Barrabas sent Nanos and Hatton to the concealed CAT 900 with the few surviving loyalists. They'd done what they had to. Held off the NKA and diverted them from White Ridge Island.

Barrabas had no doubt there was skirmishing going on over on White Ridge, but he knew that Billy Two would be evacuating many of the Kormorellois, including the king, to get them back to the mainland while hell was bursting all around them.

If there was a chance, Nanos was to radio the chopper for assistance—a possible way out. If not, the only way out was horizontal.

Barrabas and O'Toole might be able to make it to the CAT 900. But first they had to stay behind to take some of the fight out of the NKA troops converging on their location.

The NKA raiders seemed to be finding their courage now that there were fewer loyalists to deal with. But few of them realized they were about to go face-to-face with Nile Barrabas.

14

The NKA troops combed through the jungle, sometimes passing within a few yards of Barrabas and O'Toole, but then they would wander back through the morass of rain forest.

Dargient's NKA didn't have any special forces units that excelled in jungle warfare. They just had a hell of a lot of "force," and it was all coming Barrabas's way.

An umbrella of shade concealed Nile Barrabas and Liam O'Toole as the NKA troops stormed through the jungle, beating the bushes for them.

The green-faced mercenaries sat back-to-back, shrouded by tendrils of vines and wide fronds and leaves that blended with their camouflage paint. They were sitting at the base of a thick trunk, from which branches spiralled upward in competition with trees on both sides that were reaching up to the sun.

Each man covered a wide perimeter.

A half mile south of their present position they'd wiped out a ten-man patrol of Sudanese mercs and NKA regulars that had been tracking the exodus of islanders who'd moved out with Nanos and Hatton.

That had attracted every patrol in the area, who quickly converged on the spot. Although Barrabas and O'Toole wasted no time in abandoning the kill zone, they hadn't been able to move too far before seeing patrols crisscrossing this section of jungle.

It was only a matter of time before one of the patrols caught up to them.

Now the two men were cut off by NKA troops who had two thoughts in mind. First, getting out of the jungle alive. Second, collecting the bounty that Dargient had placed on the heads of the SOBs.

"Colonel," O'Toole said. His voice was flat, matter-of-fact. Gone was the camaraderie of the "boys": they were men at war.

"What is it, Liam?" Barrabas said, looking at the Irishman, who looked like a bit of jungle come alive with a crown of vines and brush forming a halo around his head and shoulders.

"I think we might be taking a fall here," he said.

Barrabas shrugged. In the distance they could hear the approach of their pursuers, whose passage through the jungle masked the low voices of the two mercenaries. It was a steady *switch-switch-switch* sound, the sound of brush being pushed aside and occasionally of men tripping over lassolike vines on the jungle floor. Sometimes there was so much noise of troops blundering through brush, it sounded like the rythmic flick of a fan—a fan whose blades were getting closer and closer.

They were getting crunched by the superior numbers of the NKA.

Barrabas had tried raising Nanos on the transceiver, but so far there had been no response.

Once the other team reached the CAT 900—if it hadn't been discovered yet by the NKA—Nanos and Hatton might have a chance to get to safety with the handful of islanders.

But Barrabas knew both of them well enough to realize that they wouldn't leave the others behind of their own accord.

They would wait for Barrabas and O'Toole, or they would come back for them. And then they all might die on the island.

"You think you reached your last stanza?" Barrabas asked. He studied the Irishman who'd been with him since the beginning of the SOBs, when he'd recruited the army captain and stopped him from getting lost in bars and in the arms of a procession of women.

"I guess maybe," the battlefield bard said. There was no fear or fatalism in his voice, just a matter-of-fact sadness. They'd fought around the globe, picking up teammates along the way and inevitably losing a few. But the core had remained the same for a while now. They'd developed into a single entity. Six SOBs. One mutual purpose. They could almost read each other's minds, knowing that someone was covering their back when they made a move. Looking out for each other and expecting the other to always be there was as natural as breathing.

Throughout it all, O'Toole had maintained his struggle with his muse. He'd written several books of poetry, many of them fashioned through his Gaelic sensibilities and cured through vats of whiskey. But the epics remained unread. He hadn't even made a splash in that world, although he'd come close. But it looked as though opportunity for everything had run out.

"It seems a damn shame to run against the brick wall here in the middle of Absolute East Nowhere," O'Toole said.

"There's one thing in our favor, Liam," Barrabas said.

"There is?"

Barrabas nodded.

"Well, I ain't going any where right now, Nile. I got plenty of time to hear the good news."

"If we do buy it," Nile said, "Heaven can't be too far away. We already got one foot in paradise."

O'Toole scanned the primitive surroundings. "No argument there," he said. "This island looks like a regular Garden of Eden."

The Irishman paused for a moment, listening to the sounds of the jungle. "If there is a heaven, you think we'll get in, considering our trade and all?"

"Hell, yes," Barrabas said. "I got connections."

"I believe you do, Colonel," O'Toole said. "I believe you do. Come heaven or hell, I'll follow you anywhere. And you can take that to the cosmic bank."

Barrabas laughed softly. "Well, if we do go out, Liam, I'll leave it up to you to provide our last words. But for Christ's sakes, go out with something that rhymes. I never did go for the free-verse stuff."

"You got it, Colonel," O'Toole said, and just as he did, he saw Barrabas's gaze harden.

Coming up from the south were a half dozen NKA raiders, their voices booming in the jungle. The SOBs exchanged glances, then O'Toole eased away about ten yards, moving slowly. No need for both of them to get wiped out in case they caught some concentrated fire.

They waited.

In a while a face peered through the brush at the edge of the kill zone. The soldier suddenly fell silent, almost as if he were aware that he just passed through an invisible curtain.

It was an NKA guerrilla, his face streaked with camou paint, looking brutish. He was a killer, but he wasn't in his milieu. More for him the jungles of the streets.

Satisfied that no one was going to take his head off, the guerrilla stepped closer.

Others joined him. They moved loudly but haltingly through the jungle. Their automatic weapons swept in wide arcs, ready to seek out and fire.

They came right toward Barrabas.

Nile watched the point man twenty yards away. He thrashed through the brush, then paused ten yards away. His steps crashed through the undergrowth. He was getting closer, coming right for Barrabas. Five yards. Three yards. Still he saw nothing.

Barrabas exhaled slowly, his silent breath sounding like a river inside of him.

The man looked his way.

Barrabas tightened his finger on the trigger, but the man moved on.

Barrabas relaxed.

The NKA herd passed them by, all of them poking into the brush randomly and jabbing their barrels, hoping to find a connection with living flesh.

They moved on out of sight.

It would have been a piece of cake to take them all out the loud way, Barrabas thought, but he and O'Toole would have given away their position.

Barrabas exhaled all the way. They were safe for a while. Their ability to sit tight while the enemy went gunning through the neighborhood for them bought some more time.

But not much.

As the patrol that had just thrashed by them reached the outer range of Barrabas's position, another NKA patrol came the same way, practically following in their footsteps.

Barrabas cursed his luck. The law of averages was working against them. Soon the forest would be full of NKA soldiers, and one of them would trip right over them, or snare their feet on the connecting wire to the Claymores that Barrabas had planted on the sides of a shallow gully.

SIMON DARGIENT had a prize. He was crouched over a wounded man stretched out on the sand, lifting the young native's shoulder to see his face.

A deep cavern of red from a machete slash had opened him along his side, splitting ribs and flesh.

He'd been chopped by the wicked blade after he'd been wounded in an ambush and had managed to crawl away. But he crawled in the wrong direction.

A half dozen NKA troops had dragged him through the rain forest. He was trying to hang on, but he was slowly fading from a gaping chest wound.

"You're dying, son," Dargient said.

Then he glanced around at the Sudanese and Tanzanian mercs and some roughshod NKA troops. "These men want to make your death painful. And they can. But you'll still die."

The man's eyes widened as he looked around and saw the vengeance-minded faces of the mercenaries.

Dargient continued. "Talk to me and I'll make sure you won't suffer."

The young man looked up, made a strained sound and nodded his head.

His agony was great enough, and the thought of any more was too much for his shocked body to comprehend.

"Is the commander of the loyalists on the island?" Dargient asked. "Is he the one we have trapped up there?"

The man nodded.

"What is his name?"

He gurgled and gasped, having trouble breathing as the blood poured out of him. But he was able to speak. He voiced one word. "Barrabas," he said.

Dargient cocked his head, surprised, then looked back at the jungle where his troops were combing through the brush. He knew the name, knew of the man's reputation, his troops, the people who worked with him. The SOBs. Soldiers of Barrabas.

The son of a bitch had blazed a wider path across the African continent than Dargient had. And now, somewhere in the wilds of Maku Island, Dargient had the great Barrabas trapped. Soon he would have his head on a stick.

The mercenary looked down and nodded approvingly. He stepped back, swiftly drew his Browning Hi-Power and pulled the trigger. The shot smashed through the wounded man's temple, turning his head sideways and planting his mouth into the ground, sowing it with a dark splotch of red.

Dargient holstered the weapon, then motioned the NKA troops back into the forest. At the same time he commanded the NKA radio operator to send a message back to home base, telling the general to come out and join the victory celebration.

NKA FIRE RIPPED through the jungle, coming straight from the second patrol that was approaching Barrabas's position.

But it wasn't aimed at him.

It was aimed at fellow NKA troops.

Apparently the point man in the new patrol had noticed movement from the stragglers in the previous patrol and had fired without thinking. But he managed to hit his target.

As the distant NKA straggler screamed and fell, the oncoming patrol opened up on them with a barrage that knifed through the forest.

As soon as they were fired upon, the first patrol whipped around and returned fire. Bullets scythed through the jungle, slicing through leaves, vines and thick tree trunks, but doing little damage because everyone had quickly sought cover.

There was a lot of shouting coming from both sides.

Barrabas and O'Toole sat in the middle of it.

During a lull in the shooting, Barrabas heard one of the men from the first patrol bellowing out, "Don't shoot! NKA! We're NKA!" The man was emerging from concealment, accompanying his words with frantic, wide sweeps of his arms that was meant to be noticed.

The man was just in hearing range of Barrabas, but as yet out of range of the oncoming patrol. Soon the other NKA troops would hear him clearly.

Barrabas slung the Sterling on his battlefield harness, then gently picked up the Model PM sniper rifle at his feet and sighted on the NKA soldier.

He exhaled, ridding his chest of most of his breath. He steadied the rifle, then pulled the trigger. The first shot took him down. Barrabas squeezed the trigger again. Then he dropped down, swiveled around, and squeezed off three rounds in the other direction.

With the momentary calm broken, both NKA patrols started firing at one another again, with Barrabas and O'Toole joining in whenever they found a target.

A hail of bullets, wood splinters and flesh and blood splattered through the rain forest as the patrols fought one another.

"Thanks for the ringside seat," O'Toole said, watching the new patrol move forward. In the thick foliage, they seemed to glide across the jungle like a tangle of dismembered torsos, arms and faces. They were coming right for the SOBs position.

As they drew closer, the oncoming NKA soldiers realized they were shooting at some of their own.

Five yards away from Barrabas, one of them suddenly shouted wildly, "It's us, it's us!"

It *was* you, Barrabas thought, drilling him at nearly point-blank range a moment after the wild-eyed NKA soldier discerned Barrabas's shape.

Barrabas continued firing at the oncoming patrol while O'Toole, back beside his friend once again, concentrated on the other patrol.

When ultimate chaos was reached and the NKAs were running around in panic, Barrabas clacked the Claymore mine, sending a maelstrom of steel balls through the jungle gully the soldiers had run through.

"Let's move," Barrabas said, clapping the Irishman on the shoulder, figuring that at any moment now the place would be crawling with NKA troops.

As they started to drift from their position they heard the heavy beat of metal wings. The Nightfox was droning over the treetops.

Nanos had managed to raise the helicopter pilot on the catamaran's radio and summoned him from White Ridge Island. That meant that Hatton and Nanos were probably going to make it out alive, and Barrabas and O'Toole just might join them—if they could get to a clearing that wasn't crawling with NKA.

They scrambled through the jungle, cutting in and out of the tangled corridors of forest, hopping over vines and fallen trees, hurrying to a patch of clearing they'd previously scouted out.

There was no way the Nightfox could land, but with an NKA army closing in on them, Barrabas and O'Toole were willing to learn how to fly.

Barrabas fired a flare straight up in the air to mark their position.

They waited, hoping for the best. And to add some backup to that hope, they loaded fresh magazines into their weapons.

THE BLACK NIGHTFOX soared overhead, stripping the upper branches of the treetops as it opened up with the 7.62 mm machine gun. It had four thousand rounds and it was shooting hell out of a line of NKA soldiers heading toward the clearing.

A stream of fire from the chopper bit into the earth, kicking up tufts of grass and dirt as it did. Split seconds later it bit into the bodies of the NKA soldiers.

They fell like a line of stationary targets, knocked off their feet by the hellish fire from above.

The Nightfox banked, then ripped into a second swarm of soldiers, who dived for cover in all directions.

SIMON DARGIENT RAGED LIKE a madman.

It was for real this time. Right after he'd sent for the general to come to the island, the trapped mercenaries were getting away.

He was screaming orders as he and Gerard Montfort urged the NKA mercs into the jungle, into the mouth of fire from the helicopter.

Dargient was practically kicking the NKA troops, pushing them ahead to be a living wall of protection for those advancing from behind.

Montfort kept up with Dargient's furious pace but couldn't help questioning him. "What's the matter? The chopper can't land up here. There's no way Barrabas can get out!"

Dargient glared at him. "You willing to bet your life on that?" he said.

Montfort paled. He'd been part of Dargient's inner circle, but he recognized that the captain wasn't making an empty threat. He shut up and followed him.

THE NIGHTFOX HOVERED above the clearing, dropping a Special Purpose Insertion and Extraction line from the cabin. The thick S.P.I.E.S. line uncoiled like a khaki snake as it dropped from the helicopter toward the ground.

Barrabas and O'Toole rigged the line to their harnesses, roped themselves side to side, and then suddenly went airborne as the long extraction line hoisted them in the air.

As they neared the treetop level surrounding the clearing, a stream of khaki-clad NKA regulars burst into the open.

O'Toole triggered the Daewoo automatic shotgun, blasting twenty-four rounds of 12-gauge slugs down into their midst. Barrabas hosed the edge of the clearing with a full clip from the Sterling gun.

A moment later they were sailing through the air, suspended from the helicopter as it banked to the right. They swung like a single-minded pendulum over the tangled greenery below.

The Nightfox soared in the direction of the coastline, bringing them out to rendezvous with the CAT 900 that was racing across the sunstruck ocean.

A few minutes later they caught up with the catamaran, and Nanos idled the high-speed boat while the chopper hovered above it.

Compared to their extraction from the jungle, the drop into the catamaran was like a walk in the park, with the SOBs and islanders easing them from the rigging.

The helicopter flew off, shadowing the CAT 900 as it roared away to freedom. Next stop Grand Kormorelle.

While the CAT 900 roared over the ocean, O'Toole looked with fondness at the dwindling size of the heavily forested island. "Paradise, my ass," he shouted. "That was one sorry hell of a place, Colonel."

"Oh, I don't know," Barrabas said, thinking of O'Toole's promise to go out with a poem on his lips. "It could have been verse."

15

General Zahim braved the sea wind as the sleek maroon Scarab 38 KV catapulted out of Port au Général. The twin 400 HP stern-drives rocketed the high-performance boat over the waves, quickly catching up to the two lead boats that just left the harbor.

Port au Général was still undergoing repair, but most of it was functional.

Zahim planned to devote more time to it as soon as they crushed the island rebellion, which would be any time now.

He stood in the cockpit like a proud figurehead, holding to his imposing cap.

There were four NKA regulars in the high-speed craft that generally served as the general's version of a royal yacht. There were five men in each of the two powerboats riding just ahead of him. Even at sea he traveled with a bodyguard.

The Scarab hull hammered through a mountainous wave, enveloping the craft in a cascade of seawater. His statuesque pose was ruined by the spray drenching his uniform, and General Zahim cursed and self-consciously sat down in the cockpit seat. But no one seemed to notice it. At times like this the general was virtually invisible. The crew preferred silent laughter to a spur-of-the-moment death sentence.

Even with the discomfort, Zahim was in high spirits. The leaders of the rebels had been cut off, and their ragtag army of islanders was cut to shreds. Dargient had radioed the general to come at once, to share in the great victory.

It wasn't his fighting ability that would count, but his image. If Zahim landed on the island and popped a few rounds skyward, twenty years later legends could be told of how the general personally led the attack on the rebels.

But his musings about the birth of a legend were abruptly cut short by the appearance of a Nightfox helicopter. It was hovering over a string of fast-moving boats in the distance.

The NKA fleet, Zahim thought at first, returning from rounding up the rebels.

But the helicopter wasn't attacking those craft. Instead, like a bird of prey spotting its quarry, the Nightfox streaked toward the Scarab and its escorts.

It swooped down on the lead boat and opened fire. The first burst from the helicopter smashed through the windscreen, knocking the crew off their feet. Then it swept in from the side and strafed the second speedboat.

General Zahim became frantic. "Turn back!" he shouted to the man piloting the Scarab. "Turn back!"

Zahim looked behind him and saw the small loyalist fleet silhouetted against the horizon, some of them bearing down on the southern end of Grand Kormorelle, others streaming toward the port.

The Scarab darted for the harbor at full speed, whining across the water at nearly sixty knots before the pilot cut the engines to guide it to the dock.

As soon as the Scarab nosed against the dock, General Zahim scrambled onto the deck, jumped from the boat, and ran down the dock, hell-bent for the presidential palace.

THE CHURCH BELL RANG with machine-gun clangs as automatic fire ripped into the bell tower.

A squad of Kormorellois, inspired by their warrior caste members, stormed uphill, firing wildly at the NKA guards in the tower. They poured an equally loud barrage against the front walls of the palace.

They'd landed earlier at the south end of Grand Kormorelle after Billy Two had evacuated them from White Ridge. Now they were striking while the NKA was in disarray.

But most of the damage was done by the Nightfox that swept above the rooftops of Korvois. Then it dropped like an angry wasp and poured machine gun fire into the front courtyard of the presidential palace, obliterating the stream of NKA troops who were standing behind the outer wall awaiting the loyalists.

Douglas Mann spun the chopper in a 180-degree turn and darted down to pepper the palace entrance with 7.62 mm projectiles.

He followed the chain-gun attack by firing a 70 mm rocket into the main hall, sending columns of stone collapsing onto the floor.

"THIS WAY!" the general shouted, waving his right arm forward, gesturing for the handful of NKA troops to cross the cobblestone road—a road pockmarked with 7.62 mm ruts.

The NKA soldiers saw loyalists everywhere they looked, pouring lead up and down the wide boulevard. Rather than charge through the barrage to the presidential palace, they took cover and returned fire against the loyalists. If Zahim wanted them to storm the palace, he was going to have to lead by example.

The chopper returned for another run, strafing the center of the road.

General Zahim continued shouting orders, but he was ignored. In the middle of a battle, the words of a fool were the first to be drowned out.

A line of NKA troops dropped against the outside wall of the church, firing point-blank range at the advancing loyalists.

More Kormorellois loyalists poured up the street, the numbers swelling as they moved from house to house.

The "returned ones" of the brotherhood had truly returned. Once again the warrior cult was on the march. They carried spears, arrows, knives and submachine guns. Their faces were streaked with war paint, and they wore talismans to protect themselves, lizard-claw necklaces that hung around their bared chests like dog tags.

As Zahim watched the growing horde, it looked like a parade of islanders from centuries past, all of them assembling for this one final battle.

They ran headlong toward the church.

From the docks below, both NKA troops and loyalist soldiers were arriving, back from the battle of Maku and White Ridge.

The battle raged all over Grand Kormorelle, and General Zahim was in the middle with nowhere to go.

The general stood on the edge of the cobblestoned street, walking in a daze.

In the crowd thronging toward him he saw a familiar face, the face of the man who was leading the loyalists toward the presidential palace.

King Daoud had returned.

Zahim stared at the half brother who had inherited the reins of power, the half brother who'd always been favored because the blood of the islands ran in his veins, while Zahim was the product of a marriage with a European wife.

"Daoud!" he shouted with impotent rage at seeing how the populace followed him blindly and as if he had earned their loyalty.

Zahim's attention was caught by a tall warrior carrying a crossbow while many of the brethren carried their primitive long bows. The tall man was in war paint, and seemed foreign. American perhaps. He was much taller and his skin wasn't the copper color of the

Kormorellois. He had to be one of the mercenaries the king had summoned.

King Daoud saw the general when a line temporarily parted between the two rulers.

Zahim saw the tall mercenary level the crossbow. But he didn't shoot. Instead the mercenary said something to Daoud, and the king grabbed a longbow from one of the brethren. He took the lengthy spearlike arrow.

Zahim froze. He fumbled with his holster, clawing for his Beretta 92SBF. The 15-round 9 mm magazine had always given him a feeling of power before. But that was power wielded against unarmed citizens.

Now the power was fleeting—it was there, but he had to wield it in the face of a man who was trying to kill him.

He thought of a way out but there was none.

He was expected to act. Everybody was watching him, and an electric anticipation filled the air.

King Daoud's gaze was unflinching as he fitted the arrow into the bow and pulled back the bowstring.

Zahim cleared the pistol from the holster, slipped his hand around the grip—

The double-edged spear sluiced through Zahim's chest, the razor-sharp spearhead emerging from the other side, pulling him back like a magnet hauling him to the ground. He fired the Beretta, but the one shot he'd got off thudded into the cobblestones.

Zahim fell, feeling the sunlight wash over his face one more time before the light started to dim and his blood ran in the streets of Korvois.

There was a loud roar from the crowd as they followed the returned king into the courtyard of the presidential palace. Both the loyalists and the warriors alike had recognized the all-important thing that would keep Daoud in the palace. He'd proved himself in battle.

The blood of kings ran in his veins.

SIMON DARGIENT LEVELED his M-16 at the white-walled church and triggered a full-auto burst. The bullets flicked through the wood in dotted-line patterns that scattered the people inside.

Some of the Kormorellois had sought refuge from the fighting there. Others had found a concealed position to fight Dargient's troops.

They found death instead.

Corporal Gautier stood beside Dargient, adding his M-16 to the fusillade. Several other NKA soldiers joined them on the run, legging it up from where their boats had gathered in the harbor.

They fired alternately at the presidential palace, to pin down any reinforcements, and at the church itself.

A loyalist with a Sterling submachine gun darted out of the church in a crouching position, firing as he ran. Gautier knocked him off his feet with a short burst, then resumed firing at the wooden walls of the church.

The fallen man was still alive and reaching for his weapon, which had skidded down the marble walkway. Gerard Montfort ran forward and stood over him like a technician of death. He split the fallen man's skull with a point-blank burst, then whipped a full-auto volley across the front of the church.

One of the NKA soldiers, a local man who'd been dragooned into service, ran up beside the mercenary captain while Dargient was firing another round churchward.

"But you are shooting into the house of God!" he shouted.

Dargient laughed. "Shoot him, too, if you see him."

The man glared at him.

"They haven't got a prayer," Dargient said. But right after he spoke, he knew it wasn't true. He moved to the edge of the rubble-strewn avenue and looked down at the port. NKA troops were pouring ashore at a steady clip. But they weren't enough. Not at the moment.

A good number of them had been left behind on the island, tied up by the guerrilla tactics. Many of the NKA were still splayed in the jungle where they'd fallen, their bloodstreams swimming with insects, their bodies attracting the feral creatures of the rain forest who'd come to claim the gifts the gods dropped into their lairs.

Now, with General Zahim dead and King Daoud firmly in control of the palace, in reality the NKA could do no more.

Grand Kormorelle was a total loss.

It was controlled by Daoud and a solid contingent of the warrior caste, many of them supported by the people of Korvois, who'd had more than their fair share of life under Zahim's rule. The Kormorellois had realized that they had to make their stand right now. There would be no second chance if they didn't seize the moment.

Dargient knew the pattern well. If he stayed here, he'd be cut down sooner or later. Trapped by the islanders.

He had to seize *his* moment.

"Corporal," he said to Gautier. "Leave some regulars here to fight a holding action. Gather the rest and put them in jeeps, cars, trucks, boats, whatever you can find."

"Where we going, Captain?" he said.

"To the nicest hotel in town, Corporal," Dargient said.

16

"Here they come, Colonel," O'Toole said. "Loaded for bear."

O'Toole handed the binoculars to Barrabas, who was sitting next to him on top of a knoll overlooking the quarter-mile bridge on the Mirror Island side. Behind them, covered by the gently inclined knoll, was a courtesy van with the sky-blue logo of the hotel emblazoned on the side.

But courtesy was the last thing in Barrabas's mind. He had a different kind of welcome for the NKA.

"Looks like he's giving it everything he's got," O'Toole said. "Just like you figured."

"Dargient's got no choice," Barrabas said, looking through the glasses. "This is the only weak spot he's got left to attack. And it's the spot we've got to defend."

Gray clouds of dust and smoke billowed from the convoy approaching the bridge on the south end of Grand Kormorelle. The lead vehicle, a three-quarter ton Rover, was nearly on the bridge when it suddenly pulled over to the side of the roadway. A roofless jeep pulled up alongside it, and the occupants talked to the men in the Rover.

"Think they suspect something?" O'Toole asked.

"Even so," Barrabas said, "they've gotta come to us. If not, they'll get hammered from the other side."

The afternoon sun beat down on them, baking the dust and grime on their weathered faces and on their tattered khakis. Both men were exhausted from the nonstop fighting in the jungle and the trek by boat back to Mirror Island.

To their left the white sand beach of The Island hotel was practically deserted. Gone were the crowds of sun worshipers sprawling half-naked on lounges, sipping fancy and exotic concoctions from long straws.

In their places were Kormorellois loyalists with weapons by their sides, ready to drop their role of sun worshipers when the NKA arrived. The loyalists had good leadership available to them. The SOBs were in charge of separate groups of the Kormorellois.

After they'd hung up the NKA troops on White Ridge and Maku, the joint exodus from the islands had brought most of the loyalist fighters to the Mirror Island and Grand Kormorelle.

Upon arrival, Barrabas had split up the SOBs, assigning Billy Two to help Daoud's troops hold down the palace.

Nanos and Hatton were in the CAT 900 idling in the hotel marina, along with a half-dozen other cruisers manned by well-armed Kormorellois.

Claude Hayes was handling security at the hotel, with responsibility for keeping the guests out of the line of fire, and commanding a line of snipers on the upper floors of the hotel.

Barrabas and O'Toole were handling the bridge detail and the islanders on the beach.

The procession started up again on the other side of the bridge as the jeep swung into place, followed by the Rover.

"Time to move," Barrabas said, putting the binoculars down, then picking up the Sterling Mk5.

O'Toole picked up a different weapon entirely, a small black box that was propped up next to his Daewoo hole-puncher.

THE BRIDGE over the Bay of Glass offered some of the most striking scenery in all of the islands. But the men who were waving automatic rifles, submachine guns and pistols might as well have been crossing a desert instead of the glittering bay. The only view they cared about was whatever came in range of their gun-barrel sights.

A stream of high-performance boats rode parallel to the convoy on the bridge, carrying the remnants of the NKA armada.

A violent glee circulated among the mercs and NKA regulars. Until now the hotels had been off limits. Today that all changed. It was open season on tourists, or as Dargient had promised them, it was "Parabellum Party Time."

BARRABAS STOMPED on the gas pedal, screeching the hotel's transport van onto the roadway leading to the bridge.

He'd waited until the high-speed convoy committed itself, until most of their vehicles were on the bridge. Now with the jeep bearing down on him, Barrabas spun the wheel sharply to the left, metal crunching on metal as he wedged the van into place.

Barrabas pushed the left side door open and jumped out of the van. Carrying the Sterling SMG, Barrabas ran to the end of the bridge.

Simultaneously Liam O'Toole pressed the button on the black box, activating the explosives he and Hayes had planted on the bridge. It wasn't a randomly executed plan.

O'Toole had spent days on the beach sketching the bridge like many a good tourist. But it hadn't been to simply please his creative urges. The sketches revealed the key impact points to place the charges that now went off with an end-of-the-world roar.

The first blast ripped the middle of the bridge, turning it into a concrete fountain as huge chunks of metal and stone flew into the air. Steel-and-concrete pillars collapsed, dropping the middle of the bridgeway into the ocean, transporting a half-dozen vehicles to the bottom.

On the Mirror Island end of the bridge, the jeep leading the convoy smashed into the van at full speed.

The driver flew out from behind the wheel, his outstretched arms flapping wildly as his head punched through the van's windshield.

While his khaki-clad body ran red with blood, hanging from the van like an ornament of war, Simon Dargient rammed the Land Rover into the assembled wreckage and managed to push it off the bridge.

The other charges went off, ripping the side spans and crumbling the roadway as a few more lead cars smashed into one another with a metallic shriek.

A few of the vehicles had made it through the barrier. Most of the others dropped into the water.

Atop the knoll, Barrabas opened up with the Sterling SMG, and O'Toole fired the shotgun. Several of the loyalists who'd been waiting for the right moment joined the fray.

Meanwhile at sea, the NKA armada was lining up to pass through the reefs. But instead of cruising easily into the bay they met a flaming wall of resistance.

Safe passage into the harbor depended on knowing the reefs and the markers. It also depended on the absence of gasoline-soaked fishing boats in flame, like the ones Nanos sent shooting out toward the gaps in the reefs like floating torpedoes. They smashed together in a hissing and roaring wall of flame.

Nanos zigzagged the CAT 900 behind the wall of fire while Hatton and four loyalist soldiers picked off the crewmen of the NKA boats milling about. Some of the NKA vessels crashed through the barrier of flame, then raced for shore before their boats caught on fire and exploded. All along the way they had to run a gauntlet of automatic fire.

SIMON DARGIENT LOOKED straight ahead as he bore down on the road leading to The Island Hotel. He looked straight ahead because the man riding next to him, the man who used to be Corporal Gautier, was throatless and eyeless, the remnants of his head resting on his blood-soaked chest. He'd been hit by a full burst of fire at close range.

They had traveled together for years now, and Dargient considered that even now perhaps they were traveling along the same path, with Gautier for once forging ahead of him.

A furrow of blood ran across Dargient's left shoulder, gouged by a slug that had chewed through his flesh before burrowing into the seat behind him.

He'd picked up his share of wounds from metal and flying glass, but it wasn't enough to stop him. He had a single purpose in mind. Reaching the hotel.

Capturing potential hostages was only part of it. He'd been outguessed and outfought every step of the way by Barrabas. But his last remaining goal of reaching the hotel would not be thwarted.

Barrabas had tried to stop him. Therefore he would reach it, come what may.

The Rover was pockmarked with bullet holes and smeared with the blood of those who had been crushed beneath its wheels. It was a gasping, straining heap of metal, and about forty yards from the hotel it gave out.

He hopped out of the metal carcass and stalked toward his destination.

Gunfire hissed through the air around him. The NKA troops who'd landed were fighting up and down the beaches, heading for their target. But Dargient walked on, oblivious to the danger and seemingly made immune by some inner rage and determination.

The tall wraith stalked down the street, carrying a French-made 9 mm MAT49 submachine gun designed for shooting from the hip. He'd planned to use it for room-to-room sweeps through the hotel.

He fired off several bursts as he walked, chasing away the shadows ducking and running behind hedges. In the high tower ahead of him he could see tourists flocking to the windows, as if this were some show put on for their entertainment.

There were snipers working from the windows, too, dropping men all around him. But Dargient moved, heedless of the fire, as if there were a psychic armor cast about him.

He moved down the avenue, close to the hotel entrance. The sun beat down on him. His lips were parched, and there was a dryness around his eyes as if he'd walked through too much fire.

He stopped in front of the entrance, where a wide bank of solid glass doors gave access to the hotel. Using the MAT49 as a key, he fired a quick burst at two of the middle doors, then stepped through.

An elevator door opened just as the Frenchman stepped into the deserted lobby, and he fired off a burst even before his eyes registered who was in the elevator.

Two loyalist soldiers dropped to the floor, their guns clattering together harmlessly.

A woman screamed. She'd been hiding in the well of the elevator car behind the control panel. There was a male voice telling her to shut up.

Jackpot! Dargient thought. *Tourists. Civilians.* Either they'd been trying to flee, or the loyalists were escorting them to another safe berth.

It didn't matter. They were there, and so was Simon Dargient.

But the door started to slide shut. Dargient flew across the lobby and smashed the heel of his palm against the button.

The door jerked back open.

"Come out!" Dargient said. "Or you get the same treatment as they did."

A blond woman came out, openmouthed with awful fear. She was young and pretty. Valuable, he thought. With her was a man who looked as if he had just landed on an alien planet and seen a threatening life-form.

"He's going to kill us!" the blonde said.

"A distinct possibility, madam," he said, enjoying the terror that distorted her pampered face. She'd been all made up to go out when the shooting started.

Dargient guided them away from the elevator with the barrel of the MAT49.

"Captain Dargient!"

The Frenchman turned his head because something about the imperious call clued him in that fate had come to meet him. Seeing a man with coarse white hair holding a Sterling SMG on him, he kept the MAT 49 trained on his tourists.

"Barrabas!" he said, and his eyes sparkled feverishly, his voice that of a magician who'd just conjured up a spirit. The spirit of death.

"It's over," Barrabas said.

"For some," Dargient agreed. "And it can be over for some more." He jerked his head toward the man and woman who were trembling against the wall. "Drop your weapon or I'll kill them."

Barrabas studied the woman's face. She was looking to him for help. The man was staring up at Dargient, moving his lips, stammering...

Barrabas stepped back.

"Do it! I won't kill you. I just want to negotiate."

As Barrabas took one more step back, Dargient demanded, "Now! Or they're dead."

Barrabas threw the Sterling to the floor.

Dargient spun around, cradling the MAT49. He fired—just as Barrabas pushed his way back through the glass door.

A barrage of 9 mm bullets shattered the glass, the loud tinkling of glass mingling with a shocked bellow of pain from Barrabas.

Dargient ran forward to confirm his kill.

Barrabas picked himself up from the ground where he'd fallen and rolled on the cement, a spine of blood-tinted shards of glass protruding from his legs. He slammed his back against the wall, beside the door he'd just thrown himself through.

Barrabas's right hand darted to the shoulder holster under his left arm. His thumb tripped the Velcro holster catch as his fingers wrapped around the grip of the 9 mm stainless steel pistol. He could hear Dargient's footsteps thumping across the floor. It was the sound of death running on broken glass.

There was no time to set himself. No time to think. Just time to act.

Barrabas pulled the pistol free and clear, heavy and solid in his hand as he spun to the right.

Dargient hurtled himself through the doorframe—his surprised eyes immediately locking onto Barrabas, his arm whirling the MAT49 around.

Barrabas punched him in the chest with the barrel and pulled the trigger. A geyser of blood sprayed onto the barrel, and at the same time, Barrabas's left hand swatted the barrel of Dargient's SMG down and to the side.

Dargient's momentum carried his legs forward, while the bullet knocked his upper body back. He managed to squeeze the trigger of the MAT49, and the bullets chewed into the ground.

Barrabas fired once more even as the Frenchman fell in a blood-spouting arc. The second bullet drilled into his forehead, and his lips emitted a last frenzied shout.

It was over. Barrabas looked at Dargient as he lay in a bloodied, crumpled heap, and shook his head. Then he reached down, and gritting his teeth, pulled out some needles of glass from his legs.

Straightening wearily, Barrabas stepped back out into the street where the SOBs were mopping up the last wave of the NKA regulars whose bodies were now littering the avenue like the bloody debris of General Zahim's coup.

Up in the windows of the hotel, Barrabas could see the tourists shouting and cheering, waving their arms.

Daoud was back on his throne. King or president or whatever he chose to call it, he'd earned it this time.

Barrabas walked up the avenue, and paused for a backward look at The Island Hotel. The top floors of the hotel appeared to be unscarred, the mirrorlike windows shining brightly in the sun with a promise of continuation.

He headed for the beach to start rounding up the SOBs.

They had come to the end of their role on the island. The islanders and the warriors had come into their own once again. They were serving a king that deserved to be followed. And that was the victory that counted.

Also, there was the larger picture. Daoud would deal with the West. The NSA monitoring station could become a reality.

They'd improved the chances for democracy in this part of the world. They'd also made it safe for the bankers and the tourists and the resort developers—though Barrabas didn't much care for that, but he knew it was important for the islands' solid economy.

Barrabas wiped his dry mouth, looking back once more at the hotel shining like a diamond in the brilliant wash of light.

It was too bright. The time had come to get the hell out of paradise.

MACK BOLAN—THE EXECUTIONER, America's supreme hero, strikes out with a dynamic new look!

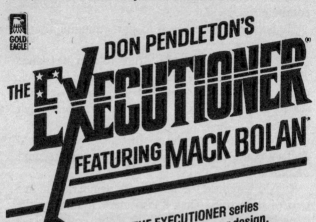

DON PENDLETON'S
THE EXECUTIONER®
FEATURING MACK BOLAN™

Beginning in September, THE EXECUTIONER series features a new, bold and contemporary cover design. As always, THE EXECUTIONER books are filled with the heart-stopping action that has thrilled readers around the world for the last 20 years.

Available wherever Gold Eagle books are sold.